EMBRACE

Happiness

*The Art of
Conflict Management*

ALI SOLEYMANIHA

iUniverse LLC
Bloomington

EMBRACE HAPPINESS – THE ART OF CONFLICT MANAGEMENT

Copyright © 2014 Ali Soleymaniha.

All rights reserved. No part of this book may be used or reproduced by any means, graphic, electronic, or mechanical, including photocopying, recording, taping or by any information storage retrieval system without the written permission of the publisher except in the case of brief quotations embodied in critical articles and reviews.

iUniverse books may be ordered through booksellers or by contacting:

iUniverse LLC
1663 Liberty Drive
Bloomington, IN 47403
www.iuniverse.com
1-800-Authors (1-800-288-4677)

Because of the dynamic nature of the Internet, any web addresses or links contained in this book may have changed since publication and may no longer be valid. The views expressed in this work are solely those of the author and do not necessarily reflect the views of the publisher, and the publisher hereby disclaims any responsibility for them.

Any people depicted in stock imagery provided by Thinkstock are models, and such images are being used for illustrative purposes only.
Certain stock imagery © Thinkstock.

ISBN: 978-1-4917-2957-1 (sc)
ISBN: 978-1-4917-2958-8 (hc)
ISBN: 978-1-4917-2959-5 (e)

Library of Congress Control Number: 2014905316

Printed in the United States of America.

iUniverse rev. date: 04/25/2014

Contents

List of Figures vii
List of Tables vii

1 INTRODUCTION 1

2 THE LIFE 4
   2.1 Equilibrium 4
   2.2 The Dao of Life 6

3 WHAT IS CONFLICT? 15
   3.1 The Conflict 15
   3.2 The Definition 20
      3.2.1 The Difference 23
      3.2.2 The Negative Emotions 28
   3.3 Myths 32

4 SOURCES OF CONFLICT 47
   4.1 Communication 50
      4.1.1 The Communication Process 50
      4.1.2 Semantics 66
      4.1.3 Cultural and Individual Differences 71
      4.1.4 Effective Listening and Observation 74
      4.1.5 Overview of the Communication Process 82
   4.2 Structure and Organisation 84
      4.2.1 Responsibility Overlaps 86
      4.2.2 Incompatible Targets 89
      4.2.3 Limited Resources 91
      4.2.4 Uncertainty in Responsibilities 93

5 ROOTS OF A CONFLICT 95
5.1 The Reality 96
5.2 The Goal 100
5.3 The Way 101
5.4 The Overview 103

6 MANAGING THE CONFLICT 104
6.1 A Look Back 104
6.2 Manage or Resolve? 107
6.3 Conflict Management Styles 108
6.3.1 Avoiding 109
6.3.2 Competing 111
6.3.3 Accommodating 113
6.3.4 Compromising 116
6.3.5 Collaborating 120
6.4 Dos and Don'ts 124
6.4.1 Avoiding 126
6.4.2 Competing 128
6.4.3 Accommodating 132
6.4.4 Compromising 136
6.4.5 Collaborating 142

7 THE CONFLICT MANAGEMENT PROCESS 145
7.1 Overview 145
7.2 Change Management Process 151
7.2.1 Unfreeze 153
7.2.2 Shape 157
7.2.3 Refreeze 161

8 CONCLUSION 164

9 BIBLIOGRAPHY 166

10 INDEX 169

List of Figures

Figure 1. Tai Chi Symbol: The Yin/Yang Equilibrium 6
Figure 2. The Worldview: The Interpretation of Reality 23
Figure 3. The Spiral Nature of a Conflict 30
Figure 4. The Environments around Us 32
Figure 5. The Wheel of Emotions 41
Figure 6. The Communication Process 50
Figure 7. Realised Strategy 159

List of Tables

Table 1. Conflict Style: Avoiding 127
Table 2. Conflict Style: Competing 131
Table 3. Conflict Style: Accommodating 135
Table 4. Conflict Style: Compromising 141
Table 5. Conflict Style: Collaborating 144
Table 6. Conflict Style: Overall Summary 147

1

Introduction

"It is your eternal responsibility to be successful and live happily; life is yours to enjoy."

By now, you might be thinking about tearing up this book and making a good use of it, to start a fire with it and bake a potato for yourself. At least that would make you happy!

With a cursory look around, you can find very successful people enjoying enormous salaries and huge houses. "How in the world can they earn so much, while I am working day and night and always ten steps behind? I am still struggling with my rent, for heaven's sake," I might consider miserably.

There are also many people enjoying their happy lives, even with little money, with their amazing families and cordial children. *They must be faking it, surely; it is not possible to be happy like this. How probable is it that your wife actually smiles at you? I mean, actually being gentle and respectful. And just look at those kids. I don't know how often he beats them that they are so well mannered,* I think wistfully.

If, by now, you have managed to start the fire and put the poor potato in it, then it is now well cooked, and you can start peeling and eating it with absolute joy. If, by any kind of miracle, you have chosen to continue reading, we are about to embark on a journey together to find out more about *happiness*.

We are going to discover the root of success, and then we will boil the root with enough water, drink it, and live happily ever after.

Ah, if only it were that easy.

I want to share an insight with you, a deep understanding of *the way*: the way to happiness, to success, to high achievements in your business and in your life. It is not a complicated path; it does not require you to do incredible tasks or sit by yourself on top of a high mountain. You just need to practice and live the way of nature: *the Dao of life*.

Through all the years I worked to develop this idea, I had many opportunities to share it with other people. Observing the revolutionary changes in their lives and professions, I have come to this belief: everybody is capable of producing such changes in their lives. It is just a matter of will; you can achieve what you thought was impossible. It will not be easy, but it will be attainable.

By the way, it is much like the times when the good doctor gave you a lollipop and said, "Don't worry; it is just a teeny tiny needle. It won't hurt a bit." Down it was going, and it hurt a lot, every time!

Therefore, I am not going to lie. Some of the topics are a bit drier than others, and I will set them aside for the time when we have gained some distance from the harbour. Considering this gap, you cannot jump off the deck and swim back.

It would be much easier to discuss some how-to remarks and provide case after case of different solutions, but this is like giving someone a cooked fish. It is imperative to learn how to fish. You will eventually catch your first fish, although small at first. You will develop the knowledge and skills gradually. That is why I believe it is essential to go through the foundations.

The Dao of life cannot be taught; you cannot put the whole complex meaning of it into words; rather, you should practice it. Throughout this journey, we are going to discover the way.

> You must *live* it in order to find and absorb it.

It is not a target we are seeking, nor a destination; it is the way on which we are marching. Our knowledge and awareness will start small, but it will gradually grow. It is like a spiral moving upwards and outwards. It will glow brighter on each step. At first, you will see tiny sparks in the dark, but going up the spiral, you will see blazing lights.

> The way is like a *spiral*, moving upwards and outwards.

Let's set sail together.

2

The Life

2.1 Equilibrium

I have been always fascinated by the way that nature manages itself. Putting humans aside for now, the rest is a pure, viable, complex system in which everything has its particular place and purpose. From the movements of atoms to the dynamics of constellations, from a single bacterium to a complex living system, all elements of nature are in complete harmony with each other. Every element performs its defined purpose – no more, no less – and plays its role perfectly in the circle of life.

Throughout this complex system, everything operates with fine precision and absolute care to the total equilibrium, except us, the humans. We believe ourselves to be the most intelligent creatures known in the entire universe. Nevertheless, we purposefully and deliberately defy all the rules of nature. We over-consume, pollute, occupy, restrict resources, and destroy them, yet nature still tries its best to rectify the wrongdoings and repair our handiwork.

The monitoring and control systems that nature uses to manage this astonishing harmony have been mostly obscured from human minds, but they have proven to be amazingly effective and efficient. Even if a single element performs outside its defined duty, it will be eliminated rigorously with absolute prejudice.

All the components of the entire system work perfectly towards a shared purpose: *equilibrium*. Every component that defies this eternal law will be quickly persecuted and eradicated.

Nature has no mercy towards outlaws. Either you maintain the equilibrium, or you will be wiped out. Even a simple rock in the way of a river flow will be rounded up to allow a smooth passage or will be destroyed to pieces.

What nature has in excess is time; it can wait for a considerable long time, but at the end, it will preserve and maintain the equilibrium.

> Nature's eternal goal is to maintain the equilibrium.

Nature is full of movements, and myriad changes occur every second: from small movements of electrons to huge eruptions of volcanoes. Actually, every single element in nature is moving, yet Mother Nature somehow manages to maintain the equilibrium. The circle of life seems to be eternally viable, if not excessively mangled by humans.

From cold to hot, up to down, famine to abundance, soft to hard, death to birth, and so forth, all of nature is moving and yet protecting the sacred equilibrium.

2.2 The Dao of Life

Everything that exists in this universe flows smoothly between two extremes, hot and cold, day and night, fast and slow, birth and death, increase and decrease: the *Poles of Nature.*

The two concurrent and conflicting poles of nature (yin and yang) create strong force fields that hold everything in their equilibrium position. Everything moves; there is no static state in the universe; nonetheless, everything is held securely between the two poles (Laozi 400 B.C.).

Figure 1. Tai Chi Symbol: The Yin/Yang Equilibrium

The night at the extreme point of itself cannot reach further; it has to turn to the day, hence the movement of black into white, and vice versa. Every element that is trying to reach outside the equilibrium state will be drawn back by the force field of nature.

The snow can sit on top of a mountain for a while, only waiting to be melted down by the sun and flow down towards its next equilibrium state. The small water streams unite to form a river, and the more it goes downwards, the more powerful it becomes. It roars and circumvents every obstacle, seeking its equilibrium state.

It eventually grows calm and slow, when it gets near its destination. From the snow to the water, from roaring to calmness, and at the end of the way, it embraces its destiny and fades into the ocean.

The water can sit inside the safety of the ocean just for a while, only to be vaporised by the sun and begin another journey towards another equilibrium state.

This is the Dao of life: the ever-maintained harmony of nature and ever-changing equilibriums. Life is a constant move around the circle, always maintaining the equilibrium.

> Life is a constant move from one equilibrium state towards another.

By moving round the circle of life, different meanings emerge. The down defines the up, and the calmness defines the roaring.

The poles of nature give meaning to the entities and concepts. Beauty is a complex concept, gaining meaning only in the existence of ugliness. The existence of a beautiful thing entails the existence of an ugly thing in return. No one can exist without the other.

This is also the same for good and bad. The good creates the bad, and vice versa. The existence of the poor defines the meaning of the rich.

These pairs are all separate from each other and, in the same time, connected strongly together. Good and bad together create the whole. Is there any other way to understand the good without knowing the bad?

Having a strength in one area necessitates the existence of a weakness in another area. Driving fast lets you reach your destination quicker, but in the same time, it deprives you of the scenery and considerably increases the possibility of an accident.

> **❝ Quote**
>
> Think how everything is created.
>
> Therefore, one must be free, and meanwhile remember the origin.
>
> They are all born; and they grow; they are all free within the poles of nature.
>
> — *Laozi, Dao De Jing, chapter 2*

If there was only one place to go, and only one situation could happen, there would be no freedom at all. Freedom means diversity; it means difference. Being free inevitably means the existence of a difference between things, and this, in turn, entails the existence of conflicts.

> This is the Dao of life, the way of nature: being free and yet bounded by the equilibrium.

This is actually the beauty of nature. The universe is full of conflicts, and there is an overabundance of them indeed, yet the whole system is completely viable and always in equilibrium.

This is a simple example of *management through conflict*. Everywhere you look, you can see conflicting and opposing entities. For each entity, there is always an opposing party. For every male, there is a female; for each proton, there is an electron. Even these days, physicists are searching for the anti-matter as the opposed party for matter.

It is also true in a much bigger perspective: the combination of rotations and a mixture of opposing gravitational forces have held the planets and the stars in the state of equilibrium for millions of years.

That is the reason, I believe, understanding conflict and the process of managing conflict are the most valuable lessons that we, as human beings, can (and must) learn. We have to learn how to identify conflict and how to manage it effectively.

Through millions of years of evolution, Mother Nature has proven to be a harsh and an extremely serious teacher. If we want to be a part of the nature, we have to learn how to live in it.

> If you do not know how to manage
> the conflicts around you, you will be
> taught by the grand master herself:
> **Mother Nature**

We must learn how to manage the conflicts; otherwise, we have to endure the consequences. Feeling down, upset, beaten, exhausted, and weary are some punishments nature has provided to teach us the way.

We will continue to feel bad until we manage to deal with the conflict positively, or we will be destroyed by it. Like that rock in the river, it will either reach an agreement with the river flow, or perish down in pieces.

> ⚠ *Example*
>
> A husband and a wife may be in a severe conflict; he insists on having his freedom and demands her obedience. She, on the other hand, will adamantly refuse to give in. She firmly demands that he be more responsible in doing household chores. She also wants some privacy and a bit of freedom of her own.
>
> Nature will go on its course. Nothing in the universe will change to ease this couple's pain, and nothing will go out of its way to help them.
>
> On the contrary, their misery will grow deeper day after day, and the resentment will replace the long-lost affections. It will develop further until they learn to manage their conflict or are destroyed by it.

This is the bitter fact about life. It is tough, and it is not forgiving. It pushes you up the spiral, on which you have only two choices: go up the path, or be pushed off it. There is no way back, nor is there any way around it.

> Always remember:
> Nature has no mercy.

You cannot circumvent your belligerent child; it is yours to manage. You cannot ignore your bitter husband; he is there, right in the middle of your life. You have to do something. You cannot close your eyes to your stern boss; he is always there to cheer you up with his tirades.

> Now remember the first lines of this book: "Life is yours to enjoy," is it not?

It is happiness that you need to redefine and learn to achieve. In other words, life is yours, and you can choose either to appreciate and enjoy the absolute happiness it can offer, or to suffer the punishments and continuous misery of Mother Nature's classroom!

We must just find the way towards the equilibrium. Anything moving outside the equilibrium will cause pain and discomfort; it is our eternal responsibility to be successful and live happily. We are bound by the forces of nature to only two options: either to be successful ourselves and enjoy the abundance of life and the bliss of happiness, or to be wiped out by vigorous, merciless nature.

> *True happiness is to maintain the equilibrium.*

Every kind of success will bring joy to our lives. We feel incredible when we manage to achieve our pre-defined goals. It is a positively marvellous sensation to taste success.

However, this prosperity will not produce *true happiness*. We may feel joyful for a while; we may even smile like a fool while strolling in the park and enjoy the quizzical looks on people's faces! However, we move on; we always do.

After achieving a goal, we set it aside and move to another goal. This is embedded in our subconscious that we always want to move higher and achieve better things. We do not feel fulfilled with the achievement of an individual goal. Every achievement is actually a step towards the next goal.

Success pertains to the achievement of a goal; every accomplishment brings joy, but just temporarily. It will not bring true and sustainable happiness; it is not long-lasting; we are forgetful creatures.

On the other hand, achieving a goal could easily mean losing other possibilities. When you drive fast, you will reach the destination faster, but you will decrease your safety and increase the possibility of a mishap.

If you work harder, you might achieve the long-awaited promotion and an increase in your income. Certainly, the greater income will make you happy. However, you may lose many happy times with your family due to your longer times of work or the hardship you endure at work and your physical or mental exhaustion. You may not see your child growing up; you may never see her laughing while playing with you. The feelings and affections between you and your family may diminish, fading day after day while you are working hard for your boss and enjoying your success at work.

Always remember that the *whole* nature is in equilibrium, not just an isolated part of it. Nothing is detached; everything is connected to each other. True happiness comes when you are successful in achieving multiple (and many times contradicting) goals.

If you can combine business prosperity along with family success, then you are truly happy. Moreover, the most important thing about true happiness is that it is not temporary. True happiness is sustainable, long-lasting, sheer bliss.

> True happiness requires managing conflicting interests and needs.

It is not an easy task; it is actually very hard to achieve true happiness. It requires you to limit your desired targets in some areas in order to create space for other goals in other aspects of life. It is essential to be able to manage conflicting interests and needs.

How do you manage the ever-increasing burden of your job concurrent with the social and emotional needs of your family, as well as your own needs?

You have only a limited amount of time, and you have to manage it effectively to achieve success in both business and family. Managing these conflicting forces is the only way that you can experience true happiness.

This is the *art of equilibrium*: the way you decide, move, and interact with your surrounding environment, in complete harmony with nature's equilibrium.

There are so many demands from us, not only from society and the environment around us, but also from ourselves. The needs we have and the ambitions we are after demand our time and energy, as do our family and other things or people around us. To manage all the conflicting interests and maintain the equilibrium requires the *art of conflict management*.

> The Dao of life is all about equilibrium, and equilibrium is all about managing conflicts.

The world around us is filled with many conflicting interests and needs. Success in one area can easily create devastating failures in another area (or areas).

While the sense of joy caused by success in one area is temporary and ephemeral, failure, on the other hand, brings emotions and sensations that are much more enduring and long-lasting.

After years of hard work, you may achieve a promotion, which will bring joy, but after a while, the sweetness of this achievement may be replaced by new responsibilities and increased expectations, which require more time and energy from you. Meanwhile, you might lose precious time with your family. Dissatisfaction may develop between the parties and this will create an ever-increasing gap between you and your family. The feelings may grow to disapproval and even to resentment.

With your hard work in one area, you have gained transitory satisfaction in your business and perpetual resentment in your home.

With the ever-increasing demands of our work environments, it is not a surprise that many of us feel so down and depressed! Negative feelings, inner unrest, and depression have physical side effects in our body, and they also bring emotional challenges. We are growing old, not in our ages, but in our faces. We lose hair; we discover new wrinkles every morning. The pimples seem to have found a good home to spread on our faces.

However, the good news is the beauty specialists and psychiatrists are most thankful for this situation. The skin-care products are being prescribed by tons. And there are long queues of people for psychiatrists.

The forces of our environment have created a situation that most of us are drowning in multiple conflicts, and some of us do not even know that they are going down. Nevertheless, we are all going down, with big smiles on our faces.

> ⚠ **Example**
>
> One of my friends works in a very reputable consulting firm in Canada; it is one of the largest corporations in its field. The company has a motto that has been engraved into every employee: "Up or out".
>
> This is senior executives' belief that every employee must move upwards, or they will be got rid of. Nobody can choose to stay in one position for a long time.
>
> They believe if an organisation is to move forward, everyone in the organisation must move forward.

This corporate culture mentioned above will create such strong forces that will affect the social lives of employees and will create long-lasting conflicts in their personal lives.

The corporate culture has proven to be effective for the organisation, as it has become one of the largest in its sector; but what sort of costs have been endured? The costs of human lives and lost happy events and ever-increasing gaps inside families might be a true challenge to calculate.

This example demonstrates that it is not always completely in our hand to manage all aspects of our lives. There will always be strong forces that you have no part in creating, yet they will affect your happiness gravely.

The forces imposed on us may seem to be unmanageable and unbending, but nature has provided ways for the rock to reach equilibrium and not be broken down.

The only tool you have in your possession to deal with these intractable situations is *conflict management*. This is the only way you can achieve happiness and deal with conflicting interests and needs. The art of conflict management is the art of turning bad to good, misery to joy, and black to white.

3

What Is Conflict?

3.1 The Conflict

You wake up in the morning. Not having time for a proper breakfast, you grab a slice of toast from the table. Finding your briefcase and shoes, you hop towards the door and jump out to the pavement, looking to the tube station, wondering whether you could get to the next train.

You finally get to your office door, the heavenly gate to your dreams, a gate that you dreadfully open and begin your daily desk job. You can just imagine the rest of this incredible day.

Finally, it is time to go home. You gather your things and follow a very precise procedure of the modern world, consisting of walking among lots of people, fighting to catch the train, battling against the pressure in the cabin, getting off the train without getting your foot stuck in the train's door. Yet another marathon of walking out the station, and finally you can be proud, you can see the door of your home in your blurry vision. Honey, you are home!

But why in the world do you feel so exhausted? You have a desk job, not requiring you to wander around or jog up the stairs. Yet still, you feel haggard, utterly lethargic. What has happened?

Our life is crammed with overflowing conflicting interests and needs, which drain our energy dry. We may be oblivious of such overpopulation of demands around us, but rest assured. They are all there, all at work dutifully to make our life harder.

Your boss may not have answered your greeting in the parking lot, and your mind is painfully at work to find out what you have done wrong today. Your colleague may say something discomforting, the telephone rings, and so forth.

Every single sound and movement demands your attention, even unconsciously. Someone is smoking in the hallway, and the smell is irritating. The client is unhappy; he has called to protest. Your wife calls and asks if you remembered to call the kid's school and discuss some issues. The boss phones and asks if you have finished the report, which you had to do thousands of years ago.

You have not had a proper breakfast, and your belly is growling. You look at your watch to see how much further you have to wait for lunchtime. You start with the bloody report, and your colleague pops in, sits on the chair in front of you, and starts babbling about his problems at home with his wife.

The boss's secretary calls this time and says the boss is not happy at all about the delay on the report, and he is asking for another report on a different subject.

And it goes around and around. Such a joy.

With all these fantastic events, are you still wondering why you are feeling lethargic? You must be thrilled that you are still alive. Definitely, you have a sound mind and a strong body that can withstand such brute forces day after day.

Remember the rock in the river. The rock was also very rough and sturdy just before it broke down to pieces.

> **❝ Quote**
>
> The bamboo that bends is stronger than the oak that resists.
>
> — *Chinese proverb*

There is a fine distinction between bending and surrendering. Surrendering means giving up, but bending is all about flexibility and adaptation. It is about finding the best position to overcome strong winds and obstacles.

Nature forces you to bend and accept its power. Resisting against the forces of nature will only result in frustration and fatigue.

Mother Nature is a very tough teacher. We need to bend and find a way to be in complete coordination with nature and be in absolute harmony and balance.

Whenever there is a force, you can be certain that somewhere, somehow, you have stepped over the equilibrium state, and the grand master has raised his wand to teach you something.

> ⚠ *Example*
>
> It's late on a Saturday afternoon, and Sarah is waiting desperately for a well-deserved rest after a long week of hectic work. Sitting on the comfort chair, she picks up her cup of tea when Bradley jumps into the drawing room, all prepared to barge out of the house.
>
> Sarah stops her son, asking about all the drama, and Bradley explains he is going to a rendezvous with his friends.
>
> Sarah tells Bradley to be at home before 9.00 p.m. at the latest, and Bradley starts protesting against this unfair curfew.
>
> They argue for a long time. Bradley stops his mother mid-sentence and runs towards his room, banging the door. Sarah sits down, frustrated and angry, looking at her now-cold tea.

> ⚠ **Example**
>
> Mr Temple is a hard-working, responsible employee at a respected company. He has worked his way up through his six years of experience in this company and hopes to soon be promoted to a senior level.
>
> During the last few weeks, Mr Temple has been late at work for several days, and his performance has declined rather considerably. Business is tough, and the cruel competition and poor economic situation have made Mr Logan, the CEO, miserable and cantankerous.
>
> Looking at the performance charts, he finds out Mr Temple's to be the lowest in the last two weeks. The telephone rings, and his chief financial officer briefly tells him that the business's performance is going downhill. He rings off, frustrated.
>
> Mr Logan picks up the phone and calls Mr Temple. After two rings, Mr Temple answers. Mr Logan shouts into the phone that he must meet him at his office first thing in the morning tomorrow.

From early childhood and throughout our lives, conflict has played (and still is playing) a very significant role. Although we might not sense its presence, we feel the discomforts it creates. It drains your energy and makes you angry; sometimes, it even makes you imagine your boss's head while cutting the bread for your soup.

We encounter numerous conflicts while we are awake and interact with people and the outside world. Even when we are asleep, we may experience some conflicts through our dreams.

Conflict is a major, ever-present factor in our lives, from which none of us are free. We need to find a productive way of co-existence, because whatever it is, conflict is not going to go away. We have to understand and discover the conflicts around us.

If we want to learn how to manage a conflict, we first have to find it; and for finding something, first we have to figure out where to look and what to look for.

3.2 The Definition

The word "conflict" comes from the Latin *con-* (together) + *fligere* (to strike), hence, originally meaning "striking together". This simple word is the most constant phenomenon in the history of humankind, as well as nature itself, and it has been the source of long debates and subject of extensive research.

Here are some definitions:

- *Oxford Dictionary:*
  - A serious disagreement or argument, typically a protracted one.

- *Merriam-Webster:*
  - Fight, battle, war.
  - Competitive or opposing action of incompatibles: antagonistic state or action (as of divergent ideas, interests, or persons).
  - Mental struggle resulting from incompatible or opposing needs, drives, wishes, or external or internal demands.

- *William Wilmot and Joyce Hocker:*
  - An expressed struggle between at least two interdependent parties who perceive incompatible goals, scarce resources, and interference from others in achieving their goals (Wilmot and Hocker 2001).

- *Susan H. Shearouse:*
  - Conflict is when what you want, need, or expect interferes with what I want, need, or expect (Shearouse 2011).

- *Erik A. Fisher and Steven W. Sharp:*
  - At the root of all conflict is a perceived inequity in power (Fisher and Sharp 2004).

➤ *Leigh L. Thompson:*
  - Conflict is the perception of differences of interests among people (Thompson 1998).

➤ *Herb Bisno:*
  - A process of social interaction involving a struggle over claims to resources, power and status, beliefs, and other preferences and desires (Bisno 1988).

➤ *Ho-Won Jeong:*
  - A conflict situation is represented by perceived goal incompatibilities and attempts to control each other's choices, which generate adverse feelings and behaviour toward each other (Jeong, *Understanding Conflict and Conflict Analysis* 2008).
  - Conflict is manifested through adversarial social action, involving two or more actors with the expression of differences, often accompanied by intense hostilities (Jeong, *Conflict Management and Resolution* 2010).

Conflict has been defined by various scholars, and as you can see above, different terms and words have been used to define this word. Some have used the word "struggle" to convey the hardship the people feel, and the efforts they put to achieve their goals.

Another definition may focus on the interference between what one wants and what others want. Still another may concentrate on the goal incompatibilities.

All the definitions, though different in wording and the area they focus on, have something in common. They all try to convey a state of being different among two or more parties, which has caused hardship and unhappiness.

One of the best and most practical definitions has been provided by Professor Michael Dues from the University of Arizona (Dues 2010):

> **Conflict is a discomforting difference.**

Professor Dues has successfully developed a very concise definition of a very complex concept. This succinct definition provides the opportunity to look at conflict with an open mind and observant eyes, which are exactly what we need for our journey.

Based on this definition, conflict is not about struggles, battles, clashes, serious disagreements, or even goal incompatibilities. It does not need to be expressed, nor is it just about interfering needs. It is simply a discomforting difference, and therefore, any conflict has two primary components: a *difference* and a *negative emotion*.

3.2.1 The Difference

Everyone has a complex set of beliefs that shapes their outlook to the world. This outlook defines how they think and how they observe and understand the world and life. It is the way of interpreting reality, a worldview that defines our understandings and behaviours.

We all perceive the real world through our senses with our future hopes, past experiences, and current paradigm. This is like looking at the world through a camera's viewfinder with several different lenses and filters.

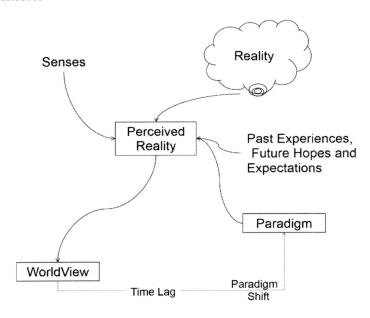

Figure 2. The Worldview: The Interpretation of Reality

Everyone's senses are different. Some may find a particular food delicious, yet others may not even be able to taste it. Some paintings are fantastic to some people's eyes, but others may see it and never understand why they love it.

It is because of this difference that we receive unique sensory information from our world. All human beings sense the world in their own unique way.

> ⚠ **Example**
>
> Just recently, I discovered one of my friends drinks espresso, only because he believes this is what intellectual people of high class drink.
>
> While I was savouring the aroma of my espresso, he was trying not to breathe and drink his down in one or two gulps, without enjoying the flavour at all.

Along with our sensory information, we also carry very important information in our memories and minds: our experiences.

These experiences create an understanding that affects our way of thinking. When we do not study for our exams, and we get bad grades, the next time we know what will happen if we do not study (and yet we never study.).

> ⚠ **Example**
>
> Yesterday was the fourth time Jack slipped on a banana peel in his driveway. Some mindless person had dropped a banana peel right in the middle of the road.
>
> Today, fortunately the banana peel was way off the middle, more to the right side of the road.
>
> Jack had to change his course to the right side not to miss it this time.

People learn in two ways. The first way is to learn from other people's experience; the second is through self-experience. Although the latter is much more expensive, it is peculiarly effective. The things we learn this way remain in our memory almost forever. It is because the lesson has been tried and tested personally, and the outcomes have been observed by the learner.

Our experiences are our invaluable lessons we have learned throughout our lives. We use our memories of experiences, consciously or unconsciously, while encountering new problems. Memories rush forward to help us avoid a previous mistake or benefit from a joyful situation.

> **" Quote**
>
> If you learn from defeat, you haven't really lost.
>
> — Zig Ziglar

Our hopes and expectations for the future may also affect our perception of the world. We may see something that we want or expect to see. The expectation makes our senses more sensitive to the information that we hope to find. In extreme cases, these future hopes may lead to a state of denial.

> **⚠ Example**
>
> A housewife may be in a phase of denial and never understand her husband's peculiar schedule. She desperately hopes for a long-lasting marriage and may interpret his late night outs as an inability to say no to his boss for overtime requests.

We, as humans, have a set of values and beliefs in our minds that governs our decisions and dictates the way we think. Each of us has a unique paradigm, shaped and settled deep inside the mind.

The paradigm is a model of the world we have built for ourselves: the way we observe the world and interpret behaviours and phenomena.

> ⚠ *Example*
>
> In my opinion, I believe children should always be the first to say hello to their elders, as a sign of politeness. They should never sit nonchalantly in front of their parents.
>
> One afternoon, we went to a friend's house for a reunion after a long absence. When we entered the room, his son was lying on the floor, talking on his phone while dangling one foot over the other.
>
> My friend did not seem to be a bit disturbed by this. He introduced his rather impudent son with obvious pride.
>
> I think my friend is much more liberal than I am. Or maybe I am as old as a dinosaur, believing in all that old rubbish mumbo jumbo.

Our interpretation of reality is affected by our senses, experiences, future hopes and expectations, and current paradigm, and every one of them is different from person to person. So it is not amazing that we find so many differences among human beings' thoughts and beliefs. Should one of these differences become discomforting, we have a conflict situation at hand. It is a difference that discomforts us.

> Conflict is not an atrocious anomaly; on the contrary, it is rather a very natural phenomenon in human society.

Although conflict is associated with bad and discomforting feelings, it is not a bad and evil thing; that understanding is fundamental in order to grasp the true nature of conflict. It is not an atrocious anomaly; on the contrary, it is a rather natural phenomenon in human society.

Conflict could happen between friends as well as among enemies. You may see two lovers, laughing pleasantly and strolling along the beach, hand in hand. It may be obscure; it may be concealed and not expressed. However, there might be a difference, which might cause a discomforting feeling, and that would be the potential seed of a future conflict.

Almost every difference between any parties may cause a discomforting feeling; hence, the overabundance of conflict. The world around us is filled with different conflicts; in fact, it consists of countless conflicts and endless confrontations.

This is the way of nature; this is what we call *diversity*. This diversity creates differences in colours, sensations, perceptions, reasoning, ideologies, theories, actions, reactions ... everything. And each difference has the potential to be discomforting; hence the conflict.

> This is the essential point:
> **the conflict is there, you just have to find it.**

A typical eye can hardly see more than a handful of conflicts in its surrounding environment, but someone trained in the art of conflict management can discover myriads and observe the complex dynamics of each conflict.

> ✅ *Practice*
>
> - Try to find as many differences as you can, between you and one of your family members (spouse, brother, sister) or a close friend.
> - Repeat this until you have discovered any possible differences between you and all your family members and close friends.
> - Now, try to identify any difference between any two of the people in your close circle of family and friends.

3.2.2 The Negative Emotions

The other primary component of any conflict situation is the stimulation of negative emotions. Conflict is a discomforting difference; therefore, it creates discomforting feelings and negative emotions. Any difference that stimulates our negative emotions causes conflict.

It is not the size or intensity of the emotion that creates the conflict; its sheer existence is enough to bring out the conflict.

Conflict stimulates negative emotions, and these emotions have a long-lasting persistence in one's mind. They are not just transitory feelings; they create wounds, sometimes deep ones, in people's spirits. Wounds will heal in time, but negative emotions have the habit of leaving long-lasting and persistent scars behind.

When a husband and a wife quarrel over some issues in their life, they often get emotional. This is the bitter fact about a conflict. Emotions are stimulated, and if people do not manage a conflict, these emotions may grow in intensity and make them say something unpleasant.

They may calm down after a while; they may forgive each other for such behaviours and words, but the bitter memory of that harsh moment will be there.

The scars will remain in their souls and remind them of the bitterness of their words and the angry looks on their face, as if they were the enemy and deserve the hatred. Some part of their minds will be blackened for a very long time, if not forever.

> Conflict will stimulate negative emotions, and negative emotions will leave behind long-lasting scars.

Emotions can grow deep and expand in intensity. At the first instance of a conflict, you may feel the emotions tickling. At the first signs of your child's peculiar activities, you may feel concerned; after a while, if you do not manage the situation, you will grow worried.

If you continue to ignore your emotions, as your body's signals for your attention, you will feel anxious. The anxiety will grow to stress and will eventually lead to an overwhelmed situation. If you still ignore the conflict, you will experience a serious exasperation.

Everything in nature moves between two extremes (yin and yang): from the blackness of the night to the brightness of the day, and from the freezing ice to the scorching heat. The movement of emotions, as well as other phenomena in nature, has a spiral characteristic.

It starts small and grows in intensity, starting from being concerned to feeling exasperated, and then it may fade down to another feeling. It may turn into sadness and start another spiral once again, going to depression and following the path towards grief and agony, and at the climax, reaching the state of misery. It will again fade down to another feeling and emotion.

It is like several circles, entangled with each other eternally. Each circle grows in size towards its climax and then shrinks back to another circle; this movement goes on forever. This is the way of nature. Everything is connected to each other in one way or another.

It goes on and on, spiral after spiral, emotion after emotion. Somewhere in the middle of one of these spirals, some emotions may cause a decision, the decision will lead to an action, the action will have consequences, and the consequence will bring another set of emotions.

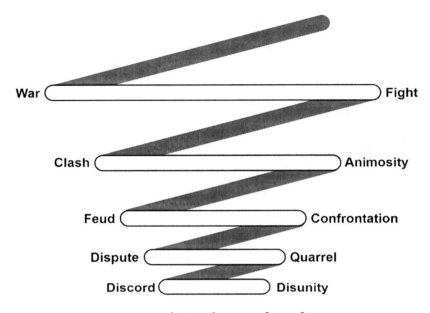

Figure 3. The Spiral Nature of a Conflict

A conflict may cause disunity between two people or groups (Figure 3). This feeling will grow deep and will expand in intensity to a discord. The two parties may have their disputes over the shared issue, but after a while, they may start quarrelling about it. This may lead to a feud and push them towards a confrontation.

The confrontation in turn might lead to a clash and a larger animosity between two parties, and a good fight may be in order if they continue on this path. The conflict may even lead to a war at its climax if the two parties fail to manage the situation and bring the spiral down to a calmer equilibrium state.

> Conflict has a spiral nature:
> it grows in size and intensity.

Nature is always in an equilibrium state. When one party's emotions grow and intensify, the other party's emotions will grow as well. When one body exerts a force on a second body, the second body simultaneously exerts a force equal in magnitude and opposite in direction to that of the first body.

Therefore, the bigger one party's emotion grows, the bigger the other party's feelings become, thus maintaining the equilibrium of nature.

If a conflict is not managed properly, it will grow to a devastating force, which will destroy its surroundings. At first, it is like a breeze, but it has the potential of becoming a calamitous tornado, turning around and forcing everything out of its place.

Therefore, it is extremely vital to understand and discover the conflict at the very first stages. It is like cancer; it develops rapidly and involves more and more people in the issue.

With each step, the conflict will create deeper emotions, which in turn will create longer lasting scars and side effects. If at least one party wants peace and true happiness, it is much better to manage the conflict at the very first steps of the spiral and not to let it grow deeper and stronger.

> ✅ **Practice**
>
> - From the previous practice, identify those differences which may cause any discomforting feeling in you or either parties.
> - For those that bother you, why do you think they create discomforting feelings?

3.3   Myths

We are living in a rapidly changing and dynamic environment in which, most of the times, we are reactive towards the events around us, rather than being proactive.

A multitude of forces are trying to shape us in their desired figure or lead us towards their chosen path. Like the rock in the riverbed, we will gradually be shaped and reshaped.

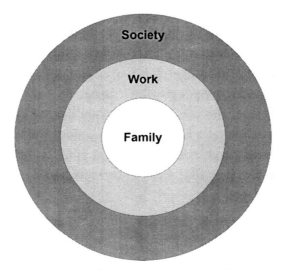

Figure 4. The Environments around Us

We have been experiencing these forces from the early days of our lives, and they have changed us and shaped us in one way or another. Therefore, none of us has a clean slate to draw upon. We have all been shaped by our own environments. We have all learned to deal with conflict in our own ways.

Family, for most people, is the first environment where they experience heartbreaking situations and unpleasant discomforts. From your early childhood, just as soon as the first time you said "No" to your parents, or even the first time you rejected a bottle of milk, you have started attending an impressively effective class on how to deal with conflict.

The way your parents answered on that day and the behaviours you have observed all along your growth, up to now, have taught you how to deal with conflict. When you had your first fight with your mates, you were lectured on Conflict Management 101.

These lectures may be delivered verbally, which might have been protracted for ages, or your parents might have preferred a more hands-on approach. One parent might have lovingly caressed you with iron fists, the other might have come later to soothe the pain and mollify your anger.

Each action or each word has been delivered zealously by your parents and was received with absolute attention by your subconscious and avaricious mind.

We learn a great deal from our families. Actually, the foundations of our current beliefs and paradigms were laid down years ago in our childhood. We have been actively learning and practicing our techniques with our friends' hair and noses, and sometimes during a conflict management session, we might find our clothes to be completely torn apart and our lips to be swollen like an apple. Those were the times we received another educational session to learn even more techniques from our older and stronger schoolmates.

Conflict Management School does not come to an end when we grow older; it just changes appearance. Our work environment creates another force field of education.

Every organisation has its own culture and code of behaviour. One firm may encourage individual leadership and aggressiveness; another may favour teamwork and closer collaborations.

In any case, we spend a lot of time in our work environment, in fact, a lot more than we spend with our own family, so that we start learning and assimilating the corporate culture.

We may rightfully think, *When in Rome, do as Romans do.* We gradually become our organisation, our company, and our work. We no longer live our lives; we actually live our works.

We try harder and harder to meet the corporate expectations, and by doing so, we unconsciously try to change ourselves to whatever the work wants; we learn how to behave the way they want, hence being reshaped and being forced to a path chosen by others.

Besides families and work environments, there is a larger community in which we live: society. Different societies demonstrate considerable differences in their culture and the way their people behave.

Regarding conflict, there is a remarkable difference between societies. Some societies are more focused on the importance of family and securing the honour of the elderly. In these societies, conflicts are not addressed directly and openly. On the other hand, in another culture, society may encourage candid and direct expression of conflicts.

Affected by the environments we have lived in, we have learned rather extensively and have been shaped by manifold forces. To transform this firmly carved sculpture, we cannot just read a book, wait for ten minutes under the sun, and hope to be cooked properly.

Every learning process needs extensive work and lots of energy and practice. We have to embrace the good things we have learned and try hard to undo some of our wrong beliefs and myths about conflict.

> **Myth #1**
> Conflict should not occur in a
> friendly environment.

You may have heard these comments: "If you love each other, there should be no conflict between you two," or "In a strong family, there is no place for a conflict." Both these comments and all other similar remarks have deep roots in our inner feelings about conflict; these feelings helped our ancestors survive: they are the survival instinct.

We have learned that each conflict has a winner and a loser, and thus, we have always seen conflict with a black-and-white filter. We had come to this belief that conflicts arise amongst enemies, those who would fight against each other, hence the belief that friends should not encounter a conflict.

It is very important, as said before, to fully understand the nature of conflict and think about it as a natural phenomenon. Actually, conflicts happen more often between friends and colleagues than between strangers.

Friends and colleagues are more interdependent, and they interact more with each other. Interaction in human society means exchanging words, actions, and emotions. Therefore, the more you interact, the more opportunity for a difference to emerge between parties, hence the more possibility for conflict to arise.

This is the Dao of life, the yin and yang at work. The closer you get, the more negative feelings occur, pulling you apart; on the other hand, the further you get, the stronger you feel longing to come back.

> **Myth #2**
> I need to be more powerful to
> resolve my conflicts.

If you were ever bullied in your life, no worries, we are all the same in our shared miserable lives. But if not, you might have been the one who was always taking my lunch at school. Thanks, pal.

Recall the "sweet" days of high school, being bullied by the massive monster classmate of yours. Can you remember the feelings now? You might have wished to be more powerful and much stronger than your opponent was, so you could test the durability of a large brick with the help of his nose.

That was one of the times we learned the sensation of longing to be more powerful. And the cartoons they produce these days are all about the same thing: giving children the invaluable sensation of being invincible and feeling the sweet taste of punching their enemy, and using lasers and missiles, and never getting blown apart.

Now that we have come to this, isn't it most peculiar that almost all the major cartoons these days are about wars and battles with extreme technologies and inconceivable creatures? What happened to all the soft emotions and beauty of the human species? How can we expect a child to learn about the beauty of collaboration, or the happiness of being with family?

As Alvin Toffler presents in his great book, *The Third Wave* (Toffler 1984), human society has gone through three distinct waves, from a settled agricultural society, which replaced the hunter-gatherer culture of humans, to the second wave of the Industrial Age society, through which the main focus was (and mostly still is) mass production and mass consumption. In this phase, the main concern of nations is making the wheels of the economy turn faster by providing incentives for more production and more consumption, and every avenue is exploitable to secure the achievement of the goals.

The meaning of *power* has been drastically changed from the first wave to the second. Once, having better lands and more crops was considered the power of a society. In the second wave, having more production capacity, as well as more destruction capability, proved to be the definition of power among groups.

The third wave of the Information Age society (according to Toffler) has reached its peak. In this wave, power is having the right information in the right time, and having the capability to manage the flow of information. Now, the meaning of power has changed once again. Muscles are still necessary and important, but there are much more important things around.

As mere human beings, we are well versed in using our muscles. We had thousands of years of evolution to teach us just that, and thanks to huge corporations, which lovingly provide our children with very educational cartoons, we all excel in the art of war. (That is completely different from the great work of Sun Tzu, *The Art of War*.)

In case of any conflict, our brain instinctively prepares itself for a life-and-death battle. Adrenaline will be pumped into the blood, heartbeats increase to send food and ammunition to muscles, and we can run faster and punch harder. Wow, what a rush.

But wait a minute. Didn't we human beings just celebrate our magnificent discovery of the possibility of *not* killing each other?

These impulsive behaviours are exactly what we must learn to unlearn. We need to nourish our brains and empower ourselves with new and more effective techniques to manage conflict.

It is true, though: the more powerful you are, the better you can manage your conflicts. But this power comes from the mind, knowledge, and perspicacity, not just the muscles.

> **Myth #3**
> For a team to be effective, they
> should all be good friends.

A group or gathering forms around mutual interests of members, like a social gathering, or a house party. People join groups that satisfy their needs, those in which they feel comfortable. Therefore, friends group together to do whatever they feel needs to be done.

Each member of the group should demonstrate the same enthusiastic feelings for the shared interests of the group. You would not join a house party, go sit in the corner, and start reading your favourite book. The group would discard you (of course, after showering you with drinks).

A team, on the other hand, is a completely different matter. Teams form to achieve certain goals, and each team member has a duty and responsibility to perform towards that shared goal. Contrary to a group, team members are selected based on their expertise and what they can bring to the table. The whole team's performance depends on covering all possible angles and different opinions, and to find the best and most effective way to achieve their goal.

Of course, it does no harm to a team for its members to be good friends, but it is not a necessity, and nobody will reject anybody from the team, because every expertise is needed for the completion of the mission.

Moreover, effective teams perform better with conflicts between their members. They use these conflicts as positive, invaluable sources of performance improvement opportunities. A *conflict positive* team is coherent and united, and members cover all possible points of view and consider every possible option.

> ⚠ *Example*
>
> The warehouse manager and financial manager of a company want the inventory level to be as close as possible to zero; this way, they can incur the minimum possible costs. Otherwise, they have to invest a lot of the company's capital to stock the shelves with goods, which might not be needed for several weeks.
>
> On the other hand, the sales manager wants the shelves to always be full. He does not want to lose potential clients just because he does not have an item they need. He wants to have all the saleable goods ready at hand, to catch the customers as they come into the store.
>
> A conflict positive organisation will form a team of these executives to find out the best inventory levels to maintain.

> **Myth #4**
> Anger is the main sign of a conflict.

It is true that anger can be one of the most visible emotional outcomes of a conflict, but it is not the only emotion being evoked. Actually, one of the major components of a conflict situation is emotion.

Conflict is a discomforting difference; therefore, it tends to stimulate a mixture of discomforting emotions. There are many such discomforting emotions; they are not limited to one or two emotions. With a brief reflection, you can name many different emotions that human beings experience.

Just start writing down every emotion you remember feeling while in a conflict situation: fear, confusion, emptiness, anxiety, annoyance, jealousy, sadness, revulsion, disgust, puzzlement, worry, loneliness, vengeance, terror, aggression, disappointment, and anger, to name a few.

The variety of these emotions is astonishing. It is amazing that a normal human being can sense and discern so many different feelings, and we distinguish them as distinctive, separate things.

In 1980, Robert Plutchik, a distinguished psychologist from Columbia University, classified human emotions into eight major groups: trust, anticipation, surprise, joy, disgust, sadness, anger, and fear. He argued that these primitive emotions are all directly connected to our most innate instinct as an animal: the survival instinct (Plutchik 2000).

Every single one of these eight feelings triggers and initiates an important activity with crucial survival implications; for example, fear sparks the fight-or-flight response to preserve our life, and joy motivates us to continue the joyful activity, whether it is eating or reproducing.

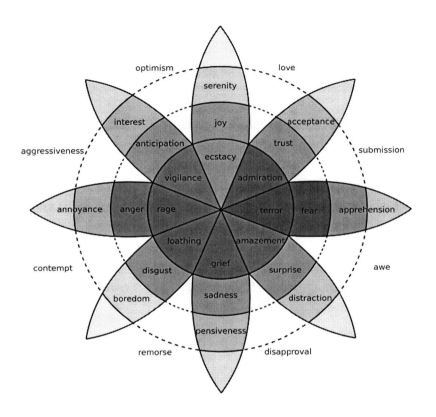

Figure 5. The Wheel of Emotions

Every other emotion is directly related to these eight basic emotions. For example, joy together with trust will create love, and anger with anticipation can create aggressiveness.

Figure 5 (Plutchik Wheel n.d.) illustrates all the emotions around a circle, in such a way that opposing emotions are sitting opposite each other, and neighbouring elements create further emotions. It beautifully depicts the Dao of life, the opposite poles of nature.

A combination of emotions are triggered in a conflict situation, from the beginning to the end. Anger is just one out of many, namely disgust, boredom, sadness, fear, surprise, terror, and so on.

> **Myth #5**
> To resolve a conflict, every difference
> between the parties should be eliminated.

Human societies are diversified; actually, all of nature is diversified. There are many things gathered under an imaginary dome. Everyone has their own set of beliefs, and it is not possible to eliminate every single difference between two parties.

The differences can be aligned or coordinated, but they cannot be erased and wiped out. Even in an absolute disagreement, both parties may agree to disagree. They can reach this mutual understanding of coexistence and peace, which can surely resolve the conflict. Therefore, to manage a conflict, it is not a necessity to eliminate every single difference.

> Conflict is a discomforting difference; hence,
> for a difference not to cause a conflict, it
> should be a non-discomforting one.

Differences between two parties can lead to a conflict, if they trigger any discomforting feelings, but this does not mean that resolving the differences will resolve the conflict. The delicate matter here is that *conflict is a one-way street*: you cannot go back and correct previous events.

If a difference initiates a discomforting feeling, and this creates a conflict between the parties, the generated feelings will have a deep impact on both parties. Going back and resolving the difference will not wipe out the after-effects. You may remember, from section 3.2.2, The Negative Emotions, how negative emotions create wounds that, even if healed, will leave long-lasting scars.

If you light a match and burn a house down, it will not do the house any good to try and put out that match.

Each discomforting difference will bring negative emotions, which, in turn, will leave deep scars. The differences may be eliminated, but having the scars is a done deal. There is no way to eliminate the wrongdoings or to wipe out any side effects the conflict created.

> **Myth #6**
> If they argue too much, they do
> not want to reach a solution.

Humans are "complex living systems" (this book is not the place to provide proof for this statement, let's just accept it as true), and a system's components perform in absolute harmony towards achieving a shared goal. Therefore, if any part of a human system does anything at all, it must have a purpose behind it. If you smile, cry, say a specific word, glance to the side, or even move your hand, for each one of them, there will be a very specific reason. Something has caused your brain to send an order to your limbs to move to a specific location or make a distinct gesture.

Every action done by a human being must have a motive. The "doer" (the one that performs the action) may not be aware of this motive, but it is definitely there. Even in extreme cases of involuntary movements, such as periodic limb movement disorder (PLMD) or Parkinson's disease, there must be a cause behind the scene. It may be still unknown to human beings, but it does not mean there is no cause. Actually, all the advancements in the field of medicine and human health are indebted to the persistence of health professionals on discovering the causes of such diseases.

Hence, it is very important to understand why people argue. People who argue have something in their minds motivating them to do so. These people truly believe in what they have in mind and are absolutely committed to the subject of discussion. Actually, the issue has such an importance for them that they cannot turn their back on it.

They are not passive and indifferent; on the contrary, they do not doubt they are right, and it is very important for them to alter your beliefs towards theirs.

These people are positively committed to the issue; the difference is that they adamantly persist in their beliefs and solutions. The issue is actually so crucial for them that they do not even bother to listen to others' opinion.

> **Myth #7**
> If the head of a team has true control,
> there will be no conflict.

Leaders with true control have the power to suppress any disagreement and control any demonstration of opposition. This means there will be no apparent or visible disagreement under their watch; the emphasis is on those two keywords: *apparent* and *visible.*

Suppression will drive disagreements underground; it will make them invisible; it will *not* eliminate or erase them. They will not magically disappear. The conflicts will hide from sight but keep growing and expanding surreptitiously.

Conflict creates discomfort and brings negative emotions; it creates unrest. A stimulated emotion cannot be dampened or be subdued by force; it needs management not elimination.

> Suppression will drive disagreements
> underground and make them unmanageable.

This is the way that an imposing power backfires, and it has been the same for thousands of years; humans instinctively tend to enforce rules and impose order as soon as they reach a higher position. This phenomenon is not limited to dictators or even depraved bosses, it is not only limited to very specific places on earth, every single one of us is well adept in imposing; we just need to find the proper person (a.k.a. the weaker one.).

Dictatorship is not an unfamiliar concept. It occurs in our families, our companies, and our societies. Every one of us has the potential to become a dictator. We just cannot see ourselves; our eyes cannot turn inside the sockets to look back at their owners.

On the other hand, our tendency towards imposing and controlling is not a bad thing. Actually, this is one of our survival mechanisms to cope with the ever-changing environment we live in; we have learned to control our surroundings in order to provide safety, shelter, and food for ourselves.

Therefore, it is natural that we feel a strong leader should control conflicts, in such a way that no disagreement would be raised; that is why history has been repeated numerous times, and it is still repeating. That is because we have not yet learned better instruments other than imposing. Nature has taught us that the strongest will survive and the weakest will perish.

The fine point here is we have paid little attention to nature. We learned a lot in the first hour of the class, but for the rest of the time, we have been in a warm bliss of a nice nap. We have to redefine and re-learn the true meaning of the word *strong*.

An ant is not a strong creature if compared to an elephant, but a bunch of ants can eat a whole elephant in the African desert. Therefore, it may be true that the strong ones win, but it does not mean being strong is the same as imposing.

As mentioned above, suppression drives conflicting parties underground and out of sight, and when they are out of sight, they can gather more troops, rearrange their forces, expand their organisation, and prepare for the next confrontation.

A leader who crushes conflicts cannot oversee the dynamics of conflict inside society or observe the arrangements of forces. Wise leaders will use freedom as a strategic tool to observe and manage their people.

> Freedom is a strategic opportunity
> to observe and manage people.

When a father has the habit of yelling at his son for his irresponsible actions, he will drive his child out of sight more and more, day after day, and yell after yell. The child will try his best to hide everything from his father. Therefore, the father will lose the opportunity to talk to his son and teach him something. This child will learn from other people and withdraw from his father as much as possible.

Sources of Conflict

Understanding the sources of conflict is an important step towards managing it. This knowledge helps you understand where to look and when to expect to find a conflict and be ready for it, before getting surprised.

Conflict is a discomforting difference, and as a matter of fact, the source of any conflict lies exactly where the difference is. This makes it very easy to know where to expect a conflict to arise, but at the same time, it brings a more complicated question: How do you identify differences?

The difference between two parties can be either *real* or *unreal*. In other words, the difference might be present in reality (the two parties have real different beliefs), or their reality may be the same but their perceptions are different.

Going back to Figure 2 (The Worldview: The Interpretation of Reality), our perception is being affected continuously by our senses, experiences, expectations, and paradigms. Therefore, for a single reality, there may be several perceived realities that are different from one another and may cause conflict, if they grow discomforting.

> ⚠ **Example**
>
> Imagine you are with a friend in a lovely, dry, and barren desert. There is no source of water except a single flask between you two.
>
> The harsh reality of the possibility of dehydration is absolutely clear to both of you. You have no more than two paths to choose from; this is a matter of life and death. You must choose which path you prefer to take.
>
> The discomforting difference is actually there; there is no misperception: it is crystal clear.

> ⚠ **Example**
>
> You have a small sum of money, and you and your wife want to invest it wisely. You learn from a friend about a stock that is expected to grow rapidly, but your wife believes it is a loser and wants to buy a different stock.
>
> In this case, the difference is rooted in your perception of reality, and your perceptions are crucially limited and are affected by your knowledge of the stocks, the market, and the global economy.
>
> Each of you has chosen a different stock based on your knowledge, and you each believe your choice is the best. The reality is the same for both of you, but your perceptions are different.

Our senses, as the effective components of our perception process, are responsible for our communication with the outer world; they help us interact with our surrounding environment. The difference in senses, from people to people, may cause a source of conflict to rise. These *communicational sources* are directly related to our interpretation of the sensory information, using our experiences, future expectations, and current paradigm: the difference between perceptions.

Moreover, there may be times when the cruel reality is the cause of the conflict. It is not the difference between our perceptions; rather, the situation in which we have been put is causing the conflict. These are *structural and organisational sources*: the difference between realities.

4.1 Communication

4.1.1 The Communication Process

Communication is as simple as shouting a word and expecting your friend to hear it, and as complex as that, as well. "Communication" comes from the Latin word *"communicare"*, meaning "to share", and it literally means sharing ideas and concepts between people.

When you communicate, you actually share information that has been formed in your mind with another person. This sharing is a process in which the intended information somehow transfers from your mind to the other person's mind.

It is a very simple yet complex process, which we perform daily with no deliberate consideration. Figure 6 illustrates the process of a one-way communication.

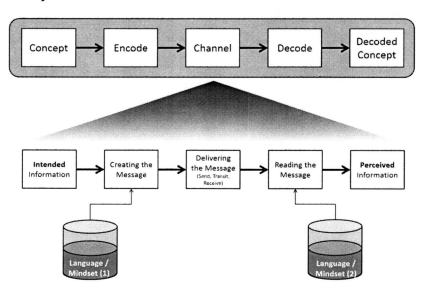

Figure 6. The Communication Process

There is a concept in your mind that you intend to convey to your friend. First, you have to use some sort of coding, the language of your choosing, and create the message.

Then, you transmit the message through a channel towards your friend, hoping for her to receive it.

After receiving the message, your friend has to use her own dictionary (language/mindset) to decode, read, and understand the message.

After that, she will perceive the information, which may or may not be the same as the intended message.

This simple process contains many opportunities for conflict. There are *noises* in the communication process that can cause a conflict in every step:

- encoding
- medium of transmission
- creating the message
- transmission channel
- receiving
- decoding the message

4.1.1.1 Encoding

This step is about putting the concept, which has formed in our minds, into a message that can be transmitted. The message can be in words (e.g. a letter), sounds (e.g. a musical composition), symbols (e.g. hand gestures, a wink), or even palpable bumps (e.g. Braille writing system).

When we encode a meaning into a message, we use a sort of conversion table (dictionary) in our mind that converts every meaning to a word, shape, sound, or a movement.

This conversion helps us bring our thoughts out of our minds and make them shareable, with the help of a comprehensive combination of words, shapes, sounds, symbols, and movements: the mixture that we call language.

Many societies have developed language systems using alphabets, like English, German, or Arabic, which they use to form words and assign meanings to these words.

Some societies, on the other hand, have developed a more elaborate system to convey meanings. They use pictures to convey the whole meaning.

These languages do not need alphabets to create words and then assign meanings to the invented words. For example, the Chinese language uses the logogram 中 to convey the meaning of "the middle, the centre", and it uses the same logogram to convey the meaning of the word "China" (中国), as in "the centre of the world, the middle kingdom".

Other than our usual language, which we use in our normal conversations, some people prefer to convey their thoughts with the language of pictures. They can paint complex concepts on blank canvases and turn them into astonishing messages.

Others may tend to use the power of sound and compose breathtaking pieces of music. Authors, on the other hand, are masters of the written language and can perform wonders by selecting and using words perfectly.

The dictionary that people use for this creation is actually a collection of their knowledge and experiences that has been formed through the years: a continuous learning process that creates and expands the dictionary.

The learning process begins as soon as we come into this world. The faces we see, and the sounds people make while looking down into the crib (while thinking of themselves to be very funny and amusing for the poor baby) all trigger very complex processes inside our magnificent brains that create different meanings and concepts in our minds.

Later on, through our day-to-day life, the information we receive through seeing, hearing, touching, tasting, and smelling, as well as other senses (e.g. sense of motion, gravity, balance, and so forth), create more experiences and bring more information for our poor grey matter to store.

The more extensive people's knowledge and experience, the more effective they can express their feelings and thoughts. A university professor can deliver a speech in a very delicate and elaborate manner. On the other hand, first graders, although able to communicate with their surroundings, do so in a much less structured manner and with much fewer words and concepts. There will be many concepts that they have not yet experienced, and for those they have, they may not yet have a comprehensive vocabulary to share with others.

Our human body can sense different kinds of raw data from the surrounding environment, and our brain has the ability to analyse, combine, and derive myriad meanings, concepts, and information from them. However, when it comes to communication and transferring the developed concepts to other fellow humans, we are not as effective as we should be (or as we think we are).

The concepts in our minds can sometimes create challenges to be encoded into a message that can be transmitted by the means we have at hand. It is not always easy to find a word to describe what you have in mind to say; in some languages, it is harder than others.

There is a wonderful info-graphic done by the design student Pei-Ying Lin, originally published by *Popular Science* (Elert 2013) in April 2013, which depicts several emotions that have specific words in some languages, but there is no word in English language to describe them.

When such emotions are in our mind, the English language lacks the ability to support us in speaking them. These emotions cannot be expressed easily, and you need to use a mixture of words in the hope of articulating your mind.

> ⚠ **Example**
>
> The German word *Waldeinsamkeit* conveys the complex feeling of being alone in the woods. It can be described as a wonderful, peaceful, relaxed, infinite, free, loving, and meditative state.

> ⚠ **Example**
>
> The Italian phrase Ti Voglio Bene means a deep emotional attachment to a family member, a friend, an animal, or even a thing.

4.1.1.2 Medium of Transmission

After encoding a message, you need to put it down in a medium for transmission. The message cannot be magically sent from your mind to another person's mind; you cannot just hold your breath and ... zzzZAP: teleport the meanings into your friend's mind. It needs a medium of transmission. (Actually, there is a fantastic idea to develop an iZAP device!)

The medium can be a piece of paper to write your message on, or even the air to send your voice through. The medium can also be your hand, delivering a caring touch, holding your friend's hand to help her cope with grief.

Any medium has its shortcomings and weaknesses; nothing is perfect. A piece of paper may deteriorate, a videotape may get degraded, a DVD may be scratched, a flash drive may be damaged, the atmosphere may distort or even lose a voice message completely due to long distances, and so on.

Considerable research is being done worldwide to enhance the durability of current storage media used to record our valuable information. Data loss is a very important subject that cannot be ignored.

If you go to an electronics store to buy a flash drive for yourself, you may find flash drives with no major physical design differences, but with considerable different price tags. Surely, the physical shape and colouring cannot create such diversity in prices.

⚠ Example

My friend and I were working on a huge project for a hedge fund management organisation; we wanted to develop a better decision model for solving financial problems. I was sure we were very productive, because we had created tons of papers filled with mumbo jumbo and equations.

After a while, we looked back at our calculations and realised it was absolutely critical to have a backup copy of the papers. The loss of those papers would really make our life miserable.

I brilliantly used a fax machine that printed on thermal papers to copy the papers and put them in my desk's drawer. We were proud of ourselves. We were so thoughtful.

After a few months of bureaucracy and market trials, our proposal reached the final phase of the approval process. We needed to go in front of the board and defend our proposal. That was when I realised I had lost the original papers. That was a perfect time for me to brag about my absolute intelligence in creating a backup copy.

Imagine my face when I discovered my critical backup copy had turned all yellow and was not readable. At least I was successful in creating a fun memory for my furious friend. I really do not want to tell the rest of the story; it is so painful.

4.1.1.3 Creating the Message

After choosing the right medium, it is time to put the intended information (now encoded) in it, a process we call creating the message. Through this process, a message will be materialised, either in the shape of a written letter, some spoken words, a recorded tape, a gesture of a hand, a wink of an eye, or any other possible alternatives.

In this process, the entity creating the message may cause some noise that may distort the whole process of communication.

Your handwriting may not be as legible as you think it is, your way of speaking may limit the intonations and stresses you can utter, or your mouth may not be able to pronounce some words.

> **⚠ *Example***
>
> One of my friends was going to a Chinese restaurant with his family and wanted to introduce his mother to the Chinese waitress he knew.
>
> To impress his girlfriend, he had worked hard to learn some Chinese words. I do not know if you have ever tried to find out the meaning of a Chinese logogram without knowing its pronunciation; believe me, it is an arduous task.
>
> By the way, the word 妈 (pronounced "Mā" – with a neutral tone) means "mother or mom" in Chinese, which my friend was planning to use. The whole sentence he was trying to say was "她是我的妈" (pronounced "tā shì wǒ de mā").
>
> I really hoped he would be able to pronounce the Chinese words correctly, because there is another word in Chinese, 马 (pronounced "Mǎ" – with a down-up tone), which means "horse".

4.1.1.4 Transmission Channel

The message needs to pass through a transmission channel to reach the recipient. This could be the postal service, the Internet, a telephone line, the atmosphere, and so on.

The channel, as well as the medium, should be chosen with absolute care. Let's say you want to send a message to your friend using hand gestures. The distance between you two, or the clarity of the passageway, such as fog in the air or trees in the line of sight, will affect the process gravely.

> One should choose the message, the medium, and the transmission channel properly for the communication process to be effective.

The transmission channel itself may be a source of noise. The air may be foggy; the telephone lines may be cut off; the post office may encounter some difficulties; postal workers may be on strike; or Iceland's volcano may erupt and postpone deliveries.

> ⚠ *Murphy's Law*
>
> Depending on your luck, the magnitude of the event can vary. You may even cause an alien invasion, if you need to send an important message to someone as quickly as possible.

⚠ Example

Technology is a marvellous thing. You can use email to send a message to the end of the world, if you need to.

Among this entire high-tech boom, there was a place I had the opportunity of living where people really understood the grave importance of transmission channels and their reliability.

For transmitting a message, they would send an email, and after the email transmission was completed, they had to call the recipient to make sure they received it.

The exact process was in place for the SMS technology as well. They used to call and check on the safe delivery of their messages. So the whole process was something like this:

<SMS>...<Phone Confirmation>...<Reply SMS>...<Phone Confirmation for the Reply SMS>... and so on.

Actually, when you think of it, technology really made the communication process much friendlier. Because this way, you are sure that you will hear your friends' voices from time to time. Don't you just love it?

4.1.1.5 Receiving

Transmission channels deliver messages to recipients. This is the fifth phase of the communication process, in which the message is received through seeing, hearing, touching, smelling, or any other alternative ways a human body can detect information.

The receiver is responsible for picking up and collecting every bit of information the channel has brought. Like any other equipment, these receivers should be fine-tuned to do their jobs perfectly with the least error (noise) possible.

The ears of a musician can pick up and distinguish very fine tunes in a large orchestra, which to untrained ears seem hardly discernible.

Our hearing ability may decrease, or our eyesight may weaken. Our sensory systems, responsible for receiving the incoming information, may grow dull and obtuse. This can be because of imprudent use (e.g. listening to loud music), improper care, or just growing old.

The receiving phase is not only about human sensors. The telephone receiver may be faulty and make noises while you are trying to listen to the other side.

Your email client may not receive the message because of a faulty firewall on your side. The email has been properly prepared and sent. The Internet backbone has done its job and transmitted the email correctly. The problem lies within your receiver, namely the computer and the email client.

continuous sharing processes from parents to children and from people to people.

A specific word has been created to be used for describing this shared concept, which is positively clear for its users (the people with the same shared concept), yet truly unfathomable to a person from a different culture.

> ⚠ **Example**
>
> My friend was telling a story about his short trip to the beautiful country of Ireland. He was a bit confused, though, and said, "I believe the only problem was everybody was selling cocaine there. I was with my family and there it was, out in the street, on every corner."
>
> "That can't be true," I said. "What do you mean exactly?"
>
> "Everywhere we went, there were people coming to us with warm smiles and asking about the crack we may have," he exclaimed, rather irritated. "Even the hotel manager came to us one evening and asked us, 'Any Crack?'"
>
> Poor chap; he must have heard people use the Irish word *Craic* a lot. Irish people are joyful and merry; they only wanted to ask if he was having a good time in their town.

There are many concepts in different cultures that can hardly be translated to another language, especially with a distinctive distant culture. Chinese, for example, is a language of philosophy and reflections in spiritual matters. There are numerous words and concepts in Chinese culture that cannot be translated very easily into English.

This fact has created inexplicable headaches for European translators trying to decode (translate) Chinese literature, especially the treasures of ancient Chinese literature.

In Chinese you do not talk the words, you rather talk the *meanings* directly. Chinese language does not use characters to form words and meanings; instead, it utilises a combination of logograms (the meanings and concepts). Each logogram, in turn, is a combination of strokes, each with their own meanings.

Many times, to understand a traditional Chinese word, there is a need to go back to the root of each word and disassemble it to its components (radicals) and initial elements.

You may find meanings that are missing in today's dictionaries, or the people who are speaking the language might look at you with complete astonishment when you describe the discovered meaning.

> ⚠ *Example*
>
> The Chinese word 無爲 (pronounced "Wú Wèi") has a very strong presence in Chinese philosophy (e.g. in Laozi's *Dao De Jing*). It has been translated to "non-action, doing nothing, or an action-less action" by many great translators.
>
> The word 無爲 is a very complex word, combining different concepts. It actually means doing nothing unless it is absolutely necessary by the laws of nature, and then, doing exactly as required, not just "doing nothing".
>
> It means actions in complete coordination with poles (yin and yang) of nature, and in true harmony with the Dao. It is completely different from "non-action".

⚠ Example

Approaching the date for the general assembly of the stockholders, I was in my office, busily checking and double-checking reports for the presentation I was to give at the meeting.

I heard a knock on my door, and before I could answer, an unfamiliar face appeared at my doorstep. I asked him politely to help himself with a cup of tea and have a seat, and then I hit CTRL+S to save my PowerPoint presentation and turned to attend to his needs.

He was a member of parliament and wanted some information, which I gladly provided. He thanked me and departed.

Almost an hour later, my phone rang. It was the chairman of the board, who was shouting on the phone and demanding that I come upstairs. (Oh God, please let me live to see another day.)

I rang off the phone and went upstairs in a flash. He asked me what I had done to make our dear MP so angry. I could not get my brain around it. I really did not recall doing anything even a little insulting. I promised to call the MP right away and apologise anyway.

I dialled his phone and apologised a hundred times before he told me that when he entered my office, I had not greeted him at once; I had continued to work on my computer!

It was only a bloody "CTRL+S"! However, apparently, even a delay of one second was insulting in his dictionary, and mine was not tuned properly for such delicacy.

4.1.2 Semantics

We humans have been using words in our daily conversations for many millennia. After years of use, language has become as natural as breathing, at least for most of us. We talk most of the time with no conscious thinking. The conversion of meanings to words happens instantly in our minds with no discernible effort, and we can talk almost simultaneously with our thinking process in the background.

This is the difference between our mother tongue and any other language we may have learned later on. The mother tongue has deep roots inside our mind, and we have been using it since the first time we opened our eyes to the world.

"Words" are defined as "single units of language which mean something and can be spoken or written" (*Oxford Advance Learner's Dictionary* 2010). Words convey meanings, and not always just one meaning; they may have different, sometimes very distant, meanings. There are different categories of words that create such confusion in our language.

Homonyms

These words have the same pronunciation and the same spelling, but they have completely different meanings. Because of the same pronunciations, these words may cause confusion in spoken communications.

> ⚠ **Example**
>
> The word *fluke* has several meanings:
>
> 1. A fish and a flatworm
> 2. The end parts of an anchor
> 3. The fins on a whale's tail
> 4. A stroke of luck

> **⚠ Example**
>
> The city *bank*. The *banks* of the River Thames. A blood *bank*. A huge *bank* of switches.
>
> *Face* of the clock. I washed my *face*. Each *face* of the cube.

Homograph

Homograph literally means "same" (homo) + "write" (graph). These words have the same spelling with the different meanings. Due to the similar spelling, these words could cause confusion in writing communications.

> **⚠ Example**
>
> Bear: the animal/to carry
>
> Minute: tiny/unit of time
>
> Row: line/argument/propel a boat
>
> Contract: formal agreement/to become smaller
>
> Incense: aromatic smoke/to enrage
>
> Subject: topic/to force a person to accept

Linguist John Higgins compiled a comprehensive list of 629 homographs in the English language (as of January 2014) on his website (The John and Muriel Higgins Home Page n.d.).

Homophone

Homophones are words that are pronounced the same but have different meanings; these words could cause confusion in spoken communications. The term comes from "same" (homo) + "voice" (phone).

> ⚠ *Example*
>
> accept/except
>
> scene/seen
>
> whine/wine
>
> ad/add
>
> aid/aide
>
> ail/ale
>
> buy/by/bye
>
> altar/alter
>
> he'd/heed
>
> Chile/chilli/chilly

For this category of words, Higgins lists 2782 words (The John and Muriel Higgins Home Page n.d.). The true meanings of these kinds of words can only be understood through the context in which they are used.

> 66 *Quote*
>
> His death, which happened in his *berth*,
>
> At forty-odd befell:
>
> They went and *told* the sexton, and
>
> The sexton *toll'd* the bell.
>
> — *Thomas Hood (Hood n.d.)*

The confusions in our communications are not limited to single words mentioned above. We use several expressions and phrases in our vernacular that convey very specific meanings for us, but they are not completely comprehensible for people from other places. This can be accentuated when parties involved in a dialogue are originally from different cultures or societies.

> ⚠ *Example*
>
> "It went down a bomb" is British slang meaning a striking success. On the other hand, *bomb* is used in American English as a "total failure'" for example, "The movie was a bomb."

> ⚠ *Example*
>
> Sandy was deep in her monitor when her boss suddenly appeared and asked her what she was doing. Having been caught off guard, she sighed and decided to be brave and tell the truth.
>
> "I am researching the recent *crash*," she answered truthfully.
>
> The boss smiled and went on his way.
>
> Sandy was shocked; being brave was not as hard as she thought it might be.
>
> The boss was very happy that his intern was working so hard to analyse the current stock market *crash*.
>
> On the other hand, the girl was preparing for gossip time at the cafeteria. She only wanted to find some details to banter about the car *crash* involving her favourite movie star.

This habit of conveying different meanings is also true not only for verbal communications, but also for the gestures we make while talking. Every movement of our limbs, eyes, nose, lips, and other parts of the body imparts a meaning to the other party; what they perceive may not be exactly what you have intended.

> ⚠ **Example**
>
> *Thumbs-up* is used in the States as a sign of approval. However, in some cultures, people may find this gesture insulting.
>
> The *beckoning sign*, used to call someone closer, is viewed in some Asian cultures as an impolite, vulgar sign.

> ⚠ **Example**
>
> A lecturer may translate your *smile* as a confirmation of his words and that you are agreeing with him, or he may think it as an impolite sneer of a rude audience.

Once realising the complex world of words and semantics, it will dawn on you that talking is not as easy as seemed before. We cannot just simply talk off the top of our heads and not use some of our well-reserved calories for our grey matter to investigate every word, and yet hope for the best in our conversations.

> It is crucial to meticulously analyse our words before we utter them and manage every movement of our body, to minimise the possibility of miscommunication.

4.1.3 Cultural and Individual Differences

Each culture is unique and can be differentiated by the differences in values, language, business practices, social norms, and other aspects. People with same culture have very specific attitudes and behaviours, which have been shaped through years of interdependent relations between them as well as with people of other societies.

These days, the once distinct borders between different cultures and societies are now blurring at a rapid pace, but you can still distinguish the amazing diversity amongst humans of this planet.

Each kind of behaviour has its own specific meaning in its society, and every gesture and way of speech has a very specific meaning that may be completely different in another culture.

Now, with ever-increasing internalisation of businesses and global movements in labour forces, these cultural differences have gained more emphasis and importance; they are one of the sources of conflict between people. Now, there is more possibility to interact with people with different cultures in our daily life than ever before.

> ⚠ *Example*
>
> In some cultures, it is common to be called by one's first name. Even in a large corporation, employees may call their boss by his or her first name. But there are cultures in which calling someone by his or her first name, unless in a very friendly environment, is considered rude, especially in a business environment, where it is considered impolite and inconsiderate.

> ⚠ **Example**
>
> In some cultures (e.g. in the Middle East), looking straight into the eyes of the opposite sex or an older family member, especially one's parents, is considered rude.

> ⚠ **Example**
>
> Some societies require people to keep a specific polite distance during face-to-face conversations, especially between opposite sexes. Standing closer may be seen as a threat of privacy and impolite.

> ⚠ **Example**
>
> In some cultures, younger people are expected to wait for the head of the family or their elders to sit first or exit/enter a room before they do. It is not acceptable for one to sit down before they do.

> ⚠ **Example**
>
> In some cultures, a table is not just a piece of wood or metal on which you can do anything you desire. It has a purpose in life. You put your foods or drinks on it; you sit around it with your family; you put your hands on it; and you use it for writing. So it is not acceptable to put your feet on the table and lean back to rest, especially in the presence of other people.

There was a time when every person we saw in our daily life was from the same society and culture. These days, if you stand in a crossroad in New York, or any other major city of the world, you can see someone from almost every possible nation and culture in the world. There are some major cities that are now almost empty of their initial citizens of ten or twenty years ago.

It is now more important than ever before to distinguish and understand different cultures around us, because no matter what our original cultures were, we have to live together and learn to coexist, and hence, create a completely new culture.

This process of coexistence has created a mixture of different people with different backgrounds and beliefs. The closer people get to each other, the more interaction occurs between them, and the greater the possibility of conflict.

We, as groups of people, are different from each other by having different cultures. We are also different from each other as individual beings. People have different characters and value systems based on the way they have been raised and the experiences they have accumulated throughout their lives.

The values that you have come to accept and believe in create a pathway through which you think, decide, and act. Those are the guidelines showing the way that help you correct your course towards the right path.

For every decision, we unconsciously consult with our value system to find out whether it is right or wrong. We will not do something we think of as wrong, and we are compelled towards the righteous ones.

Something that seems wrong to you may seem completely right through the eyes of another. A gesture or a comment by your colleague may make you go berserk. Yet still, your colleague will continue with his deed, completely oblivious of the irritation he caused.

> If you disapprove of an act or a comment,
> it does not necessarily mean that you
> are right and they are wrong.

4.1.4 Effective Listening and Observation

Communications is both verbal and non-verbal. Some information is spoken or written; other is conveyed non-verbally. For effective communication, we have to pay supreme attention to both parts.

The information sent and received through a common human communication process can be identified and grouped in three distinctive categories: vocal information, visual information, and tactile information.

For vocal information, we need our ears, and for visual and tactile information, we are dependent on our eyes and sense of touch.

We will discuss the vocal information under "Listening" and the visual and tactile information under "Observation". With a little bit of tolerance, we will include tactile information with visual.

4.1.4.1 Effective Listening

There is a world of difference between hearing and listening. Hearing depends on the working condition of your ears. It means that you have the ability to sense the sound waves coming into your ears. As soon as your eardrum vibrates, and your brain receives the signals, hearing has occurred; your ears works perfectly, and your nerves transmit the information flawlessly.

On the other hand, when these vibrations and signals result in more brain activity in parts of the brain that are related to comprehension, reasoning, and thinking, we are truly listening. Hearing involves receiving the waves, but *listening* entails understanding them.

> Listening is a deliberate act of hearing and comprehending.

When we hear, it is just our ears that are working. They absorb sound waves, the eardrums vibrate, and all the middle and inner parts of the ears dutifully do their jobs as required; the nerves also deliver the messages continuously to where they should be sent. All the hard work is to no avail, because in your head, you are dealing with your own problems. *Who cares about this miserable creature sitting in front of me, babbling like an idiot?* I might think, while my friend thinks he has found a sympathetic shoulder to cry on.

The sensing part (hearing) should result in some level of thinking in order for listening to happen. For listening, we have to hear the words and try to understand them. The more you understand, the more effective the listening process has been. Therefore, for a listening process to be effective, we must concentrate and pay complete attention to all the words that are being said.

It is not enough to just hear the words; we have to understand them. We have to think about them and comprehend the true meaning (or meanings) behind them. The words should be analysed in detail, and the context and the situation should be taken under consideration to discover the meanings of the words.

Moreover, it is not enough to understand the words; it is essential to *fully* understand what we are hearing. A considerable effort should be made not to miss any single word. People who are talking, consciously or unconsciously, select specific combinations of words to voice their opinions and thoughts. Every single one of them is crucial. It is inconsequential whether you think they are annoying, long-winded, and loquacious; you need to capture every single word.

> ⚠ *Example*
>
> I had a friend, Gabby, in high school who could be amazingly annoying if he put his mind into it. Whenever he called, I knew that I would be on the phone for the rest of the day, unless an earthquake or a volcanic eruption interrupted him.
>
> One day, I was with another friend of mine grumbling about how garrulous our mutual friend is. I said I did not know what to do when he called.
>
> Just then, the phone rang, and the caller ID showed that Gabby was on the line.
>
> "Watch and learn!" my friend said.
>
> He picked up the phone and talked to Gabby for a while, and then he put the receiver on the table, came over to me, and continued our previous conversation.
>
> Every ten minutes or so, he picked up the receiver, said, "Aha," and then put down the receiver again on the table.
>
> I was shocked by this brutal act; surely it was not ethical, was it?
>
> But it was bloody marvellous.

Furthermore, it is not enough to fully understand the words we are hearing, we have to make sure to fully understand *what is being said*, because that may be heard differently due to numerous noises in the communication process.

We have to make sure that what we are hearing is exactly the same as what has been said. It is essential to find effective mechanisms to reduce the effects of noises and ensure the accuracy of what we hear.

> Listening requires understanding
> what you are hearing.
> Effective listening requires conscious efforts
> to fully understand what is being said.

From the time the words are shaping inside the speaker's mouth, there are many noises affecting the message that is going to reach your ear (refer to section 4.1.1, The Communication Process). A word may be chosen incorrectly to represent a specific meaning or a thought; the chosen word may be pronounced differently; the voiced word may be distorted in the air before reaching our ears. Our ears may not be able to hear the word exactly, and our brain may convert the heard word to a meaning completely different from the intended one.

Therefore, it requires a considerable amount of effort and energy to make sure you have eliminated every possible noise in the way, and sometimes, it is not within your power to correct an error in the whole process.

The mindset (the conversion table) inside the speaker's head is not yours to meddle with; you can hardly do anything about their speech, intonations, accent, and the like.

> ✅ *Practice*
>
> - How could you be sure that you are hearing what is intended to be said in the first place?

4.1.4.2 Effective Observation

During the communication process, many kinds of visual information emerges from both sides: a hand gesture, a movement of the eyes, nodding, folding the hands, opening the palms, waving fingers, and the like. These are just a few examples of the many variations of visual information during a simple communication process.

Although the visual signs are indeed visual, their identification is not a simple act of looking. You may look directly at the other person but not see the signs.

Looking involves turning the eyes in a specific direction. As soon as your eyes are aligned with an object, and as long as there is enough lighting, looking has happened. The visual information has been captured by the eyes and has been transmitted to the brain.

Similar to the hearing process, the looking process is only responsible for receiving the information. As soon as the information is received, the looking process is complete.

If the received information from the looking process creates any awareness, we have *seen* the information. The seeing process makes us aware of our surroundings. This is the process during which visual perception occurs.

> Seeing is a deliberate act of looking and comprehension.

Every capturing of visual signals through the eyes is not a visual perception, it is merely looking. For seeing to happen, it is important for these signals to create awareness and develop a perception. This is a fine and complex ability that enables us to be visually aware of our surroundings.

Many kinds of visual information emerge during a communication process, and they are not one-time static signals; they evolve and change continuously. Therefore, the process of seeing is continuous and is performed over time; it is actually a watching process through which we pay close attention to the subject of our interest.

Watching is a continuous combination of looking, seeing, and understanding over time.

For effective communication, it is not enough to just watch the other person; you need to observe the other party (or parties). You need to watch every change and movement closely and comprehend the true meaning behind each change you see.

The movement or the change may be conscious or unconscious; it may even be concealed deliberately by the other party to hide their true emotions. All the changes should be discovered and understood.

> Observation is actually a discovery process.

When people talk consciously, they continuously try to convert thoughts and meanings into comprehensible words and motions. Meanwhile, their brain is working unconsciously in the background, dealing with a convoluted mixture of emotions piling upon each other in a rapid pace as the conversation goes on.

Some of the emotions may be unconsciously converted to undeliberate movements and motions. The talking person may not be aware of them, but they will be materialised, like it or not. The cheeks may grow red, the eyes may roll up, they may glance to one side, the hands may be folded on the chest, sweat may appear on the forehead, and the like.

People may learn to control some of these movements. A boy can try not to roll his eyes whenever his father is talking to him, but he can hardly control the sweat emerging on his forehead. A girl can hardly control her blushing when a loved one says hello to her in the school.

Each movement and each change delivers some underlying information, which is an invaluable source of information for an observant mind. Our body talks, but not in the same way we talk, of course. Discovering and understanding this body language is crucial for anyone who wants to manage conflict.

People may try to alter their way of speech or even use different words or accents, but body language comes from a place much deeper inside that can hardly be controlled.

Body language is much more sincere; it delivers more truth than we may want to share. We can learn to control it to some degree, but not completely. It takes too much effort and practice to master body language and to control it, and even then, there will be still some changes happening outside of our control. Our pupils may dilate, our eyes may move, our cheeks may change colour, our hands may sweat, and so forth.

Observation is a very complex activity that involves monitoring, watching, discovering, discerning, and comprehending. During observation, you monitor the subject of interest closely and watch its movements and changes carefully over time to discover underlying information, which you then try to discern and comprehend.

> Observation is a deliberate and careful combination of monitoring, watching, discovering, discerning, and comprehending.

It is crucial to understand the fine distinction between what you are looking at and what is being shown. The emerged movements and changes are visual information that come to our eyes in order to be seen. However, the things we see may not be the same as what is intended for us to see. The speaker may convert a specific emotion to a hand gesture, which may mean something completely different in our mind. Moreover, environmental noises could also distort the images we see.

> Observing requires understanding what you are seeing.
> Effective observing requires a conscious effort to fully understand what is being shown.

On the other hand, the person you are observing may try to obscure his or her emotions by controlling their movements or even deliver other movements to mislead you. Therefore, it is absolutely essential to ensure the validity of the information and our interpretation of it. It totally depends on the competence of the observer to read and validate the body language of the one being observed.

> **⚠ Example**
>
> I was in the second year of my university when we heard about a training course that was planned for our teachers. The title of the course was "Body Language". Very peculiar topic, we thought; therefore, very naturally, some of us decided to listen surreptitiously to what was presented to our beloved teachers.
>
> That day we understood that teachers should pay attention to their students, especially whether they nodded or not. "If the students are nodding, that means they are listening carefully to the teacher; otherwise, their minds are elsewhere," the presenter said, desperately trying to bring a smile to our teachers' lips.
>
> That was a very successful recce operation. From that day, we knew what to do. Whenever a teacher looked at us, we enthusiastically nodded our head, and as soon as he turned away, we would go back to our games under the tables.
>
> The poor teacher was enjoying a 100 per cent attentive class. He could not believe one course on body language could be so effective.

4.1.5 Overview of the Communication Process

Human senses are subjective and qualitative, and this makes it hard to share emotions and thoughts exactly and flawlessly. We, as human beings, depend highly on our communications skills to share and exchange information and understand each other.

Listening and observing are our crucial competences to assimilate our surroundings. Through these skills, we are able to comprehend complex meanings and thoughts during a communication process. All the words and all the movements will be listened to and observed; and every possible meaning, obvious or hidden, will be discovered and understood.

In fact, listening and observing are the most genuine ways of paying respect to your fellow partner in a conversation. Listening and observation take effort, and it is most obvious to someone talking to you whether you are paying attention or not. It will not be missed on her that you are concentrating and trying to absorb every single word she says or shows.

> Listening and observing are the most genuine forms of paying respect to your fellow partner in a conversation.

If you don't listen and observe, you will definitely miss some, if not every bit, of the meanings that are being said or shown, and that will cost you a great deal. That is because your response will not cover all the concerned issues, or even worse, you may say something completely contrary to what has been said before, and you did not comprehend it in time.

In the worst case, you may be caught red-handed. If she asked you a question and the only thing you could say was, "Huh?" you will no longer need any more tips to improve your conflict management skills; you need some survival techniques, because tonight you will be sleeping in the park. No warm food for tonight, bro.

To be an effective communicator, one needs to be an effective listener and effective observer. Although the ability to talk is necessary and needed, it is not as important as listening and observation. In fact, it is one of the first things we do as soon as we open our eyes to this world! A baby's cry is her first attempt to talk and communicate her needs.

On the other hand, these days, there are very few natural ways for babies to learn the importance of listening and observing. They do not have to listen and observe; they only have to order someone else to bring them food or prepare their shelter.

Most people no longer live in jungles, and few of them need to suffer to fulfil their basic needs of food and shelter. Once upon a time, we had to go and find some wood sticks and some rubber to make our own toys; these days, our kids are in a devastating quandary: "Should I order Dad to buy an Xbox or a PlayStation?" How harsh life can be!

The opportunities for us to learn how to listen and observe are growing smaller and smaller, in such a way that most of us are getting amazingly competent in not listening and not observing.

When we are in a deep discussion with someone, while the other party is talking passionately, instead of listening to what is being said, we are preparing our cannon to fire as soon as he or she is done talking. And while we are firing our emotionally fantastic words at the enemy's defence lines, the other person is busy measuring the gunpowder needed for the next blast: "Just stop talking, and I will blow you to smithereens!"

> **❝ Quote**
>
> To talk too much will subjugate you and makes you limited and obedient to the words you said.
>
> Listen freely, and be the guardian of the equilibrium and the balanced way.
>
> — *Laozi, Dao De Jing, chapter 5*

4.2 Structure and Organisation

Sometimes, the source of the conflict is not in the way we communicate (or miscommunicate); it is rather derived from the environment that is surrounding us. This environment might be organised and structured by a third party, your adverse party, or even yourself.

In other words, the location, structure and conditions you experience through a conflict situation could be the choice of yourself, or it may be organised by your adverse party; it may even be decided for you by a third party (other than you and your adverse party).

> ⚠ *Example*
>
> One late afternoon, you come home utterly haggard by the hard work of that day, furious with your boss for overloading you with extra paperwork.
>
> You open the door, hoping to just sit for a while and rest for a couple of minutes, when you hear your wife's scream welcoming you warmly inside. She is frustrated by your recent late comings.
>
> "Look who is finally here," she cries bitterly. "You finally realised you've got a home, didn't you?"
>
> "I was not wandering around or celebrating my glorious life in a pub, mind you!" you reply, a little dismayed.
>
> "So I must thank you for your understanding and not being a complete pillock, coming back all drunk and wobbly," she cries out loud, looking daggers at you. "And who do you think is responsible for such a glorious life? Shall I ask our neighbours? Maybe they could help us find the responsible one!"

> "I was busy at work. I am not happy either. I am tired and just need a moment to rest," you say, trying to calm her.
>
> "But I was relaxing at home with our little boy, having nothing to do, and I am absolutely happy. Thank you for asking." she retorts angrily.
>
> And on and on it goes.

In the example above, the situation and the environment of the conflict have been chosen by you and your wife. If you were more clairvoyant and predicted such conflict after one or two nights of late arrivals, you would proactively invite her to a friendly discussion during a night out. This way, you are the one selecting and organising the environment.

When conflict arises in the workplace, the environment has usually been structured and organised by a third party (e.g. the business proprietor or the manager), and therefore, the elements of the environment are mostly out of your control.

Although you may not have a great deal of control over some of your surrounding elements, it is crucial to identify and recognise them as sources of conflict. This knowledge has a considerable effect on your attitude towards your adverse party. You may realise the difference is not between you and her; it lies in the way your environment has been organised.

4.2.1 Responsibility Overlaps

One of the major tasks in the process of business organising is to assign tasks and responsibilities to individual workers in an organisation (or a household), in such a way that you ensure each and every task has been assigned, and the business whole has been secured, and in the same time, no single individual has an overlapping responsibility without a proper explanation.

Regardless of the type of the organisation, the existence of an overlap means there is at least one task for which you have more than one person or team responsible. This creates an uncertainty between parties on deciding who should actually do the job or (if they both do the job) which result will be accepted by the boss.

Every person and team has its own body of knowledge and pool of skills; therefore, each one may do the job with different approaches and may reach different results.

There is a critical distinction between overlapping responsibilities of individuals and shared objectives of team members in an organisation. Every team has an objective shared by all the team members. Every team member, in turn, has a very specific responsibility to help the team achieve the shared objective.

Therefore, sharing a task, between two or more individuals, does not create an overlap. The shared task turns into the shared objective of the team, and each team member will be assigned a definite and distinct responsibility in order to fulfil the shared task.

Overlaps cause ambiguity in an organisation. The organisation may be a global corporation or even a small family, which in itself is an organisation, consisting of family members with their defined roles, responsibilities, and relations.

If an overlap exists in an organisation, no one will be sure enough who must exactly do the job or how it should be performed. Each person may have a different mindset towards the overlapped responsibility, and everyone may prefer their own way of doing things.

This means organisers must be vigilant not to create an overlap in responsibilities, or if they should create it, they must make sure to provide organisational means and mechanisms to deal with future conflicts, which may rise from this very overlap.

> ✓ **Practice**
>
> - Why in the world would people deliberately create an overlap in their own organisation?

One of the issues mentioned above regarding overlapping responsibilities was the different approaches people may follow, and that is exactly what astute organisational architects are aiming for. They want to create a *conflict positive organisation* and gain as much as they can from the conflicts between their people, hence the need for an organisational mechanism to manage the conflicts and make sure they are in control.

No one needs a chaotic and un-predictive organisation; at least most people do not want that to happen. They want the benefits of the conflict, while avoiding the negative aspects. They want to have different approaches and cover every possible angle, while averting the clashes and confrontations that may arise between people.

> ⚠ **Example**
>
> Mr Ripley has assigned two analysts to prepare a report on the performance of their business over the past eight quarters.
>
> Mr Jones, the first analyst, produces a chart depicting a rising line, demonstrating an increase in profit figures in every quarter. Mr Ripley is positively joyful.

Ms Pierce, on the other hand, starts her presentation with a declining line, showing a decrease in the rate of increase in the profit figures.

She debates that although the profit figures are increasing, the rate in which they are increasing, in fact, is dropping, and soon the trend will be reversed, and the profit figures will start decreasing.

Ms Pierce's presentation has created havoc in Mr Ripley's dreams. He calls them both incompetent idiots who cannot decide if they are doing good or bad in the business.

"Sorry, sir," Mr Pierce interjects. "I think it is more proper if you would say 'doing well' rather than ..."

Mr Ripley starts walking towards his analyst, slowly clenching his fists.

4.2.2 Incompatible Targets

The performance targets asked from you define your decisions and work. If targets defined for two people are not compatible with each other, this will create an organisational conflict between those two. Both parties are doing their best to meet their goals, yet they are in constant friction with each other.

> ⚠ *Example*
>
> Thomas, the inventory manager, always tries to keep the inventory levels as low as possible in order to reduce the cost of inventory and trim the unproductive materials sitting in inventory shelves for days.
>
> On the other hand, Dale, the sales manager, wants the inventory to always be full to the brim. This way, he ensures that whenever a customer pops in for a product, he has it on hand and can make the deal before she goes to another store or changes her mind.

The organisational mechanism to deal with this dilemma will create the optimum level of inventory, considering the various parameters such as cost of inventory, possibility of sales, rate of sales, competition, cost of losing a customer, and so on.

> ⚠ *Example*
>
> The Internal Audit Department has the responsibility of reviewing and auditing internal procedures and paperwork to find errors and flaws in a business's internal operations. Reporting the findings to the top management

team, they have the opportunity to perform corrective actions or manage the consequences before being surprised by an outside party.

Considering the errors they may find in other departments, almost every single department hates these guys, just because they have to do what they have been told to do.

⚠ Example

The CEO has assigned his R&D team to develop new projects to push the company out of the current situation, which is like being trapped in a swamp. The operation is monotonous, and everybody is bored doing the same thing, day after day.

Two weeks later, after a serious board meeting, the CEO calls for his financial officer and asks him to start cutting costs at all departments by at least 10 per cent. The profit margin is diminishing, and the company is on the brink of bankruptcy.

The R&D team and the Financial Department fall into a fervent quarrel over the cost of the department. The R&D Department has to spend more in order to identify and develop new projects; on the other hand, the Financial Department has to limit the R&D budget and reduce costs by 10 per cent.

4.2.3 Limited Resources

Throughout history, battles have been fought to acquire resources. The earth's limited resources and humankind's greedy appetite have caused many conflicts since the beginning of time.

The resources we are after take various shapes. They may be money, land, water, food, shelter, a job, a position in your company, or even that girl in your school.

Humans are born hunters. We have been hunting for thousands of years. We have learned if we want something, we have to hunt for it, and regardless of the war wounds that we may suffer, we still go to battle within our families, workplaces, and everywhere that we find the opportunity to bang our heads to the wall. The harder the obstacles, the greater the satisfaction.

> ⚠ *Example*
>
> The different departments may fight for receiving a larger portion of the corporate budget.

Sometimes, we enter into a conflict completely innocent and with no intention of waging a war.

> ⚠ *Example*
>
> The children compete for their parents' attention and time.

Regardless of our intent, the outcome is the same: we have dived head first into a conflict-infested situation. And the source of the conflict is not me, and it is not you; it is simply that the thing we are both after is limited. Therefore, every solution you may think of should be about the resources, not anything else. The limited resources are the main reason we are in the conflict. So if we want to manage the conflict, we should not go and destroy our knuckles and noses. The solution to the problem lies around the source of the problem. We have to think about the limited resource and find out what we can do about its scarcity, or find a way to share it somehow.

4.2.4 Uncertainty in Responsibilities

Clear and precisely described job descriptions help you develop a more effective organisation (or family). Uncertainty creates workplace confusion and makes people wonder what exactly is expected from them.

If the job description has not been clearly defined, employees will always wait for the boss to speak up and tell them what to do. And because the job has not been defined at the first place, the infrastructural requirements and knowledge/skill prerequisites may not be effectively developed; therefore, the results and performances of the employees may not be as expected. The underperformance, in turn, creates new conflicts between employees and their managers. Nobody will be happy at the end, and everyone can easily accuse the other party for their low performance.

It may seem obvious to define responsibilities as clearly as possible, yet you may find it rather challenging. The ever-changing and dynamic business environment requires more-flexible and agile individuals and teams. The only way a business can survive in today's world of pandemonium is to be vigilant and adaptive. So there is an ever-increasing need for job definitions to be flexible, as well as to be completely clear and without ambiguity.

If you should define a flexible job for an individual, you have to specifically identify the job boundaries, the inputs that may be needed, and the outputs that are expected.

If doing the actual job should be flexible and the individual is to be granted the opportunity to make decisions, any required standards should be defined and clarified. You have to clearly define the output of the process (the goal) and clarify the process with which you are going to evaluate the success or failure of the job.

Agile companies today define their senior people's jobs as "black boxes," with clearly identified inputs and precisely defined outputs. The inside of the black box is all delegated to the employee to find out how to use the inputs to create the outputs. Except for some corporate rules and regulations, which must be met, employees have the freedom to create and innovate inside their black box.

As long as the corporate regulations are met and the produced output is satisfactory, no one questions the methods and techniques used by the employee to achieve the required goals. If the produced outputs are otherwise not satisfactory, there will be improvement and development processes to empower employees to achieve their goals.

> Flexibility is not the same as uncertainty.
> Flexibility requires clearly defined
> inputs and detailed outputs.

If you do not precisely define inputs and outputs in a process, you will achieve the only possible result, which is nothing more than chaos. No defined outputs leads to uncertainty, and it eventually leads to chaos.

5

Roots of a Conflict

In the previous chapter, we studied some sources that may cause a conflict. Regardless of the sources of a conflict, whatever they may be, there is always a deep root from which the conflict is feeding. Before any attempt to delve into our magic bag of solutions, we must first discover the roots of our conflicts.

For every problem to be solved, we need to find the roots that are feeding the problem. If we fail to discover the roots of a conflict situation, we cannot effectively address them, and all our efforts will not produce any satisfactory results, and the conflict may rise again and again.

> ⚠ **Example**
>
> Consider you have a beautiful tree in your backyard, and one day you realise some of the leaves are turning yellow. No matter what you do, they keep falling off your beloved tree.
>
> You call a professional to come and take care of the problem.
>
> The professional comes and asks for a ladder. He goes up the ladder and starts painting the yellow leaves with a very beautiful green paint.

5.1   The Reality

In every negotiation and every discussion, the first thing that may well act as the root of the conflict, although not visible at first, is *reality*. What exactly do we mean by this?

"To be or not to be?" This is the famous soliloquy from Shakespeare's play *The Tragedy of Hamlet, Prince of Denmark*. What Hamlet mused about long ago still is the first possible root of a conflict in human society.

Albert Einstein described reality as "merely an illusion, albeit a very persistent one." Reality is everything that we actually see or experience. But there are billions of brains and twice as many eyes!

People experience the world in their own way, and as many human beings as there are out there, there are that many different perceptions. So in each situation, different observers may perceive different realities, and that is the first root of the conflict that we are seeking.

Is it really there or not? Are we doing well or bad? Are we making profit or not? *"To be or not to be, that is the question."*

> *Reality: To Be or Not to Be?*

> ⚠ **Example**
>
> In the case of Mr Ripley, the poor guy was confused between his two top analysts. Mr Jones believes the company performance to be good, while Ms Pierce adamantly concludes the company is going downhill.
>
> The root cause of this conflict is based on the different perception of the current situation (reality). Both analysts have used their knowledge and information at hand to gain their perceptions of the current situation.

> Although the situation is in one real state, each party perceives it differently, hence the discomforting difference and the conflict.

> ⚠ *Example*
>
> Tom and Lisa, his wife, are in deep discussion. The holidays are coming, and Lisa wants to have a nice vacation.
>
> Lisa says they need two extra days for their vacation to be perfect, and it is Tom's responsibility to go to his boss and demand two more days of leave.
>
> Tom says he does not know if he can get that from his unyielding boss.
>
> Lisa presents some brochures of a nice chalet in the Alps, with a wonderful view of a beautiful lake. Tom wonders if they have enough money to even think about it, let alone go to the actual place.
>
> They can never reach an agreement while their perception of the current situation is so widely different.

Reality is relatively the easiest obstacle to overcome, because it is already there and can be discussed with no prejudice. People create multiple realities based on their own perception of the world; therefore, the number of realities present in your discussion is limited to the number of individual people involved, so it is bound to be finite and limited.

> ⚠ *Example*
>
> My wife and I are in a constant dispute. I believe my son spends very little time studying and needs to stop going out so much with his friends.
>
> My wife, on the other hand, firmly believes I am too strict and our son is studying very hard indeed and needs more fun and time out.

To overcome the conflict which has been caused by a difference in realities, it is essential to work on the root, which is the people's perceptions and multiple realities involved in the situation.

Both parties should discuss the issue in detail and provide details on how they have come to this perception and why they believe their perception is the true reality.

In the example above, my wife and I should sit together (instead of banging our heads!) and have a dialogue like proper grown-ups. I should make it clear why I think my son's study time is not enough and how I have measured this time, what enough means in my mind, and what standards I have compared his study time with.

My wife also should explain clearly why she thinks the time our son spends is enough and how she believes the quality of the time spent is much more important than the amount of time used up. She should explain why she thinks her perception of reality is valid and why I should accept that.

> The first step is to check reality and investigate the perceptions.

The multiple realities and different perceptions of the current situation is the first possible place for a conflict to emerge; therefore, for any conflict that we are planning to manage, we need to first check whether all the parties are looking at the same thing and if their perceptions are analogous.

5.2 The Goal

After you manage to reach agreement on the current situation, both parties have the same perception of the real world. Everything is ready for the next root of conflicts to emerge. By now, you know *what it is*; you want to find out what it should be or what should be done.

The question in this section is *"Shall or shall not?"* Each party may have different ideas about the desirable situation, so everybody will form and define their own set of goals to achieve, believing that this goal is the best and should be pursued.

Reality has a one-to-one relationship with each individual, meaning each individual has one and only one specific reality in mind. Unlike reality, we cannot say the same for the goals. Goals are related to the future, the future that has yet to come; therefore, it is not finite, and it is not limited.

Every individual involved in the conflict can (emphasis on the possibility, not the ability) develop several goals based on their knowledge, mindset, previous experiences, dreams, and desires.

As long as there is more than one goal on the table, there will be conflicts. So if you can identify several goals in your midst, although invisible and not expressed, you can be absolutely sure that there are conflicts in people's minds, yet to explode.

> ### *The Goal: Shall or Shall Not?*

> **⚠ Example**
>
> Tom and Lisa have finally reached an agreement. Now they know how many days and how much money they have to burn.
>
> Lisa wishes to go across the pond and visit her favourite city, New York. Tom, on the other hand, is aiming for China.
>
> They are both getting ready for another bloody round.

5.3 The Way

Once the goal is finalised, you have to decide how you want to achieve it. You have to develop a course of action to enable you to reach your goal. This very much depends on the mindset, knowledge, and experience of the people; hence, it is infinite and unlimited.

For every goal, it is hypothetically possible to develop more than one way to achieve it, if the reality was finite, and the goals were unlimited; in this case, the ways are definitely multitudinous and so much more than the total number of goals. (So you'd better surrender and accept defeat now while you are standing.)

The conflicts arise when the people involved in the situation try to find the best way out of myriad possibilities. Everyone will have their own set of criteria to evaluate each possibility and find out the best one. To have different criteria results in different evaluations and selections.

> *The Way: Which is the Best?*

> **⚠ Example**
>
> After hours of deliberation, poor Mr Ripley comes to the conclusion that the company's performance is in fact decreasing. He calls for a strategic meeting to discuss the situation.
>
> There are several suggestions on the table. Thomas believes they have to try to increase sales. This is the best way to improve the situation.
>
> Frank disagrees with him. He explains that in the current competitive market, increasing sales is not an easy task and takes more time

than they intend to wait. He proposes the best strategy for the company is to reduce costs.

Sue believes the problem lies in the company's pricing policy. She thinks they have to increase sale prices.

David sneers and says, "We are currently losing the market, now you propose to increase the prices?"

"So what is your genius way?" Sue asks bitterly.

David presents his idea to lay off some personnel to reduce costs. Frank laughs and says, "Fantastic solution! First, we can get rid of David. That way we may have a hope!"

While the team is arguing, Mr Ripley sighs and stands up to collect all the sharp items in the room out of his team's reach.

5.4 The Overview

Because the conflict triggers negative feelings, people may go emotional during a discussion and start talking about whatever they think is important and has priority.

In each discussion, the crucial task is to make sure everybody is talking about the same thing; otherwise, it is almost impossible to reach an agreement between involved parties. If everyone is focused on their own issues, the discussion will turn to separate monologues, with no hope in a foreseeable future.

The root of a conflict may be the different perceptions of reality, it may be the difference in multiple goals, or it could be the myriad ways people are proposing. Whatever the root of the conflict, it is very important to identify it as soon as possible, before emotions intensify.

The first step is to check people's perception of the current situation (section 5.1, The Reality) and make sure they are all on the same page. Before completing this phase, it is not advisable to move to the next phase.

Checking reality is the foundation of the conflict management process. We can develop a solution based on a shared and stable foundation. Without this mutually agreed-upon foundation (perception of reality), further agreements will be very hard to achieve.

The second step is to identify and clarify every single goal that is being proposed by either party. Each goal should be discussed in detail, and all the aspects shall be investigated.

After reaching agreement on the goal, for the final phase, both parties should discuss the different ways they think should be pursued to achieve the goal.

This is a bottom-up approach to manage a conflict situation. We start with the deepest root, which is reality, and work our way up towards the goal and from there towards reaching an agreement about the way.

6

Managing the Conflict

6.1   A Look Back

Ever since living creatures started inhabiting the earth, there have been clashes and confrontations. Humans learned to fight in order to eat, be safe, and survive.

This very survival instinct has been embedded deep in our subconscious. We, as humans, had to learn how to be strong and how to defend ourselves. For a long time, our bodies' muscles did the talking. The bigger and stronger you were, the better your chances on gathering some food and securing a shelter.

We had a great advantage over other species; we had something that ancient Greeks called reasoning.

Human beings found reasoning a better substitute for the brutal fights, transforming physical combats to verbal ones, hence reducing the costs and fatal risks.

It was Solon (638–558 BC) who is credited with laying the foundations of Athenian democracy; his idea helped his nation end the vicious cycles of retaliations, private revenges, and tribal battles (Bordenn 1999).

After that, others such as Thales of Miletus, Pythagoras of Samos, Socrates, Plato, and other philosophers and scholars continued to build on this foundation, developing the first adversary system.

This school of thought enabled ancient Greeks to establish an Athenian democratic justice system, in which, instead of fighting, both parties presented their case in a public court in an adversarial process with a jury and a presiding judge.

Actually, the word for "trial" in ancient Greece was "agon" ("ἀγών") (Goodpaster 1987), which means "gathering or assembly, a contest or a struggle, a dramatic conflict between chief characters in a play" (Encyclopaedia Britannica n.d.). The trial was a gathering of *dikastēs* (jurors), who listened to the cases presented by both parties, and the court decided their fates.

This adversarial system, which was the foundation of our courts today, was an astonishing achievement for humankind, yet it had several shortcomings.

The survival instinct is ingrained deeply inside. So, the concepts of winning and losing were (and still are) fundamental in the adversary system. One side would win the debate, while the other should accept the defeat.

The other shortcoming is inherent in the nature of the adversary system. The system is based on reasoning, meaning both parties have to present their case and defend it against the rebuttals of the adverse party. So whoever could argue better and present their case more effectively could raise the odds in their favour.

As a natural result of the process, the art of reasoning became popular, and a market was developed to provide such a glamorous asset. So whoever could pay could benefit from the knowledge of reasoning. The poor, who could not afford to learn such techniques, had to present their defence impotently and futilely.

This aspect of reasoning was discussed beautifully in a well-developed article from Hugo Mercier and Dan Sperber (Mercier and Sperber 2011). In this article, they articulate:

Reasoning is generally seen as a means to improve knowledge and make better decisions. However, much evidence shows that reasoning often leads to epistemic distortions and poor decisions.... The function of reasoning is argumentative. It is to devise and evaluate arguments intended to persuade.

Based on this hypothesis, reasoning is not a method to find the truth; it has evolved through years, as a means to convince others.

The method of reasoning used by ancient philosophers was called *dialectic*,[1] which means "the art of debate". This method required all the parties to discuss and debate logically, and consider all the aspects of an issue to discover the truth.

This method of reasoning has been contaminated with the engraved concept of win/lose and, according to Mercier and Sperber, has been turned to an "argumentative nature".

Each party, having its own set of beliefs and knowledge, sees the world in its own specific way and derives its distinct theories and models. While in a conflict situation, each party reasons in such a way to convince the other party towards their own beliefs, not to listen and understand the other party's point of view.

Regardless of these few shortcomings, this was an extraordinary development for our species to experience the possibilities and new ways of conflict management, although with the fall of Rome and Europe plummeting into chaos, we experienced a period of Dark Ages and instinctively understood that the sword was much more important than the pen.

It took many years and many lives for humans to settle down again and rediscover their intellectual treasures, most of them kept safe by the Church and scholars from other nations.

---

[1] (Oxford Advance Learner's Dictionary 2010): Origin: Late Middle English: from Old French *dialectique* or Latin *dialectica*, from Greek *dialektikē* (*tekhnē*) "(art) of debate", from *dialegesthai* "converse with", from *dia* "through" + *legein* "speak".

6.2 Manage or Resolve?

"To resolve" has been defined in dictionaries as an act of finding a solution or making a firm decision. However, it carries another meaning inside. In essence, the word "resolve" conveys the meaning of dissolving and disintegrating a problem to find the final solution, thus having a sense of finality.

When you find a resolution to a problem, you believe it to be final, whereas the process of dealing with conflict is usually long term and continuous.

On the other hand, management, unlike resolution, has a continuous nature. When there is a conflict, unless all the parties completely agree on all the issues, every proposed and agreed-upon solution is intermediary, and the process goes on, even if not expressed.

In other words:

> Even if there is an agreement between parties, the conflict has not been resolved yet, unless you make certain that all the parties have come to exactly the same belief.

Therefore, it seems more appropriate to use the term *conflict management* rather than *conflict resolution*. We manage the conflict, hoping to resolve it completely, but even if we cannot resolve the issue, we are still able to manage the process and the outcomes.

Conflict creates inner forces that drive our decisions and actions, both intentionally and unintentionally. The conflict itself is a dynamic phenomenon; it is a sensation materialised in a human mind. It may evolve; it may develop and expand, and it will never stop.

Therefore, the management of such a dynamic event cannot be static; rather it must be as well a dynamic and ever-changing process.

6.3 Conflict Management Styles

Conflict is a discomforting difference; it discomforts us and makes us feel uneasy. It emotionally engages all the parties involved in the conflict and causes different kinds of emotional reactions, whether they are expressed or not.

Understanding the way people usually tend to handle a conflict is an important key to learning how to manage the conflict itself.

In 1974, Kenneth W. Thomas and Ralph H. Kilmann introduced their model to describe five distinct conflict-handling behaviours. (Kilmann and Thomas n.d.)

According to this model, facing a conflict, people will present different behaviours based on two important factors. People are different from each other in two ways:

- The degree to which people care for themselves
- The degree to which people care for other people.

People who value their goals and interests the most are more *assertive* than those who care for other people's feelings and interests (and hence are more *cooperative*).

Assertive people tend to ignore other people's feelings and goals and they pursue their goals with no regard to the cost of their actions. On the other hand, cooperative people will be more inclined to sacrifice their goals and interest for the better of other people.

Kilmann and Thomas identified five distinct sets of people:

- unassertive and uncooperative (avoiding)
- absolutely assertive (competing)
- absolutely cooperative (accommodating)
- semi-assertive and semi-cooperative (compromising)
- assertive and cooperative (collaborating)

Therefore, experiencing a conflict situation, people may exhibit one or a combination of not more than five distinct behaviours: avoiding, accommodating, competing, compromising, and collaborating.

6.3.1 Avoiding

Avoiding literally means "clearing out"; it is related to the Latin word *vacare* meaning "vacate". This is an unassertive and uncooperative style. Individuals who are avoiding in the face of a conflict do not address their concerns, nor do they care about the other party's interests.

It is not that the conflict does not affect them; on the contrary, it certainly discomforts them; otherwise, it would not be a conflict. However, they have come to this idea that avoiding is the best solution to confront a conflict. They may even try to wipe out the question, instead of answering it.

There may be several reasons why they avoid the conflict. They may be afraid that dealing with the conflict may make it harsher, or it may backfire. In other words, they may feel the total cost of dealing with the conflict is much higher than the benefits.

Avoiding is not always about fearing the conflict; it may also be used as a diplomatic tactic or manoeuvre. If you try a dead end, and bump your head to the wall, you may well avoid it the second time. You may pull back and manoeuvre the situation.

> ⚠ **Example**
>
> Alice is frustrated with her son. Jack always comes home very late at night and does not listen to his mother.
>
> Roy comes home from work, and right at the door, Alice starts complaining about Jack. She tells Roy to have a word with him and deal with the situation.
>
> Jack believes that if he confronts his son, Jack will react bitterly, and there will be no more respect for him. He argues that Jack always

listens to his uncle, and Alice should rather call Uncle Morris and ask him to talk to Jack.

Alice asks her husband to call Uncle Morris himself and explain the situation. Jack refuses firmly, and says, "He is your brother, and it's better for you to call him. Besides, I don't want him to think I cannot handle the problem."

✓ *Practice*

- Write down any conflict situation, in home as well as in business, that you have avoided.

6.3.2 Competing

Competing is an assertive-uncooperative style. Competing individuals need to reach their goals, even at the expense of the other party. It is not important what happens to the other party, or whether they are happy with the results or not, as long as they are achieving their goals.

This style is based on power, so we use whatever gives us the upper hand. Nothing, absolutely nothing (in case of absolute competing), will prevent us from achieving our goals. We need to realise our goals, so back-stabbing is just a simple tool in our toolbox. It would be okay to rat our colleague out to the boss or pull the rug out from under her.

Although this style has been called "competing" by the creators of the model, it is not about competing to the end line to receive a trophy. In fact, competing is merely holding and maintaining the position that you believe is right.

> Competing is about insisting on your position and not backing up.

> **❝❝ Quote**
>
> You have enemies? Good. That means you've stood up for something, sometime in your life.
>
> — Winston Churchill

> **⚠ Example**
>
> Mr Doyle is being asked by the board of directors to prepare a report for the next weekly meeting. He puts the phone down and quickly marches to the hallway towards his analysts' cubicles.

He clears his throat to get everybody's attention. He tells them to cancel their evening schedules for the next three days. "Nobody goes home unless I am absolutely happy about the report you are going to prepare," he says rather firmly.

Nobody seems happy. Tim fearfully says he has to bring his father to the hospital for his regular session with his therapist and asks to be dismissed.

Mr Doyle tells him to decide if he wants to stay and work, or go and never come back, as he turns and marches back to his office.

⚠ Example

Alice asks her husband to have a word with their son, Jack, about his new habit of coming back home late at nights.

When Jack comes back home, he finds his father waiting grimly for him. He says hello and turns to go to his room, when Roy shouts and stops him.

Roy orders him to never again be late and always be home before it gets dark. He threatens Jack with not letting him inside the next time.

✓ Practice

- Identify each situation in which you have competed.
- Where do you mostly compete? At home, or at work?

6.3.3 Accommodating

Accommodating is an unassertive-cooperative style. In this mode, you do not value much your own needs and goals; instead, the other party's goals are highlighted and pursued. People may even ignore their ambitions and priorities in order to attend to the other party.

> **❛❛ Quote**
>
> Greater love hath no man than this, that a man lay down his life for his friends.
>
> — *John 15:13 (KJV)*

Accommodating people deliberately sacrifice their needs for the better of the other one. The root to this extreme behaviour can be traced back to either *love* or *fear*. People ignore their well-being and interests only if they love another person and for that person they are willing to sacrifice, or they fear the outcomes of them pursuing their goals.

> **❛❛ Quote**
>
> Once there was a tree, and she loved a little boy.
>
> ...and she loved a boy very, very much – even more than she loved herself.
>
> — *Shel Silverstein, The Giving Tree*

> ⚠ **Example**
>
> When a house catches fire with children trapped inside, the man of the house starts comprehensive calculations about the clothes he is wearing, or the probability of catching fire, and even the price of the suit he has on. Maybe it is better to take the jacket off before running into the fire to save his kids.
>
> He takes off his jacket and realises his shirt is also valuable; it is a gift from Aunt Fran, for heaven's sake! He takes off the shirt and looks back to the burning house.
>
> "Well, it is obviously too late," he says, "The kids are all gone! There is no use to burn myself as well.
>
> "Maybe the next time!" he continues.
>
> The mother, on the other hand, instinctively jumps inside the fire, never considering the possibility of burning or wondering even whether she can save her children or not. It is not important in a mother's mind. She will gladly die to rescue her children.
>
> This is a decision based solely on pure love.

On the other hand, there are occasions when we accommodate because of our fear of the outcome. In the workplace, if you happen to have an imperious boss, you may have enjoyed the ecstasy of life.

He may be the type who orders you around and demands more and more of you every day. Each time he demands more time and energy from you, you obey and do what pleases him. In this way, you have sacrificed your emotions, your health, and surely your family's happiness.

Accommodating can easily be excessive and extreme; you may overindulge the other party, or you may gradually lose everything you once had.

> **❝ Quote**
>
> If you set out to be liked, you would be prepared to compromise on anything at any time, and you would achieve nothing.
>
> — Margaret Thatcher

Accommodating is based on giving, and not getting anything in return. Therefore, it may easily turn into havoc, a one-way situation on which you have no control, and the only way to go is downwards.

It is very much like a spiral movement. The more you accommodate, the more people expect you to accommodate; therefore, we have to be vigilant about this style. Just like a wild horse, as soon as you release the reins, you lose all the control.

> **✓ Practice**
>
> - Identify the situations in which you have accommodated.
> - Where do you mostly accommodate? At home, or at work?
> - With whom?
> - In each situation, identify the core reason you have accommodated. Love? Fear?

6.3.4 Compromising

This is midway between two extremes: mid-level assertive and mid-level cooperative. In the compromising mode, you will not be so assertive to neglect other people's interests, and in the same time, you are not so cooperative that you ignore yours.

In the compromise, the idea is to find a middle ground between two players that both parties can accept. You are ready to give up some of your interests in order to gain some points from the other side; you give something to receive something back.

> ❛❛ *Quote*
>
> Barack Obama: "A good compromise, a good piece of legislation, is like a good sentence, or a good piece of music. Everybody can recognize it. They say, 'Huh. It works. It makes sense.'"
>
> — *William Finnegan, "The Candidate," New Yorker (31 May 2004)*

Compromise is, in nature, a bargaining process. Both parties start from a far-away position and, step by step, try to reach the middle ground. Each party attempts to draw the middle ground closer to their first starting position.

> ⚠ *Example*
>
> My friend's wife, Katey, always criticised him of not being able to bargain enough, and always paying too much. One day, she brought him on a shopping spree, as a punishment for his ignorance.

> In a boutique shop, she picked up a very nice nightdress and asked for the price.
>
> "Isn't it a beauty? I can just imagine you in this," said the proprietor.
>
> "Well, I can let it go for $880," he added with a sigh.
>
> Katey put down the gown and walked towards the man. "I can see what you mean by the beauty; that's exactly why I chose this one. I can pay you $100 for it, cash, right now," she said proudly.
>
> "I can sell it for much higher, lady. Please come back if you seriously want this dress," said the man.
>
> "I can pay you $130, no more, and that's final," Katey said, grasping at the gown.
>
> And on and on went the bargaining; it was in fact the most effective punishment for my friend. He went out for some fresh air.
>
> After ages of profuse bargaining, Katey walked out of the store, proudly holding a bag containing her purchases.
>
> "What happened inside?" asked the poor husband.
>
> "I bought this amazing dress for only $876.50. That is how you should bargain, my dear," she said, walking away utterly pleased with her spoils of war.

One of the problems with compromise is that both parties try their best to start further away, so they will have much more land to give up, and therefore ensuring their profit margin. The more points you have before the negotiations, the better you can play.

> **❝ Quote**
>
> When the final result is expected to be a compromise, it is often prudent to start from an extreme position.
>
> — *John Maynard Keynes, The Economic Consequences of the Peace*

Therefore, when being fixated on compromising, both parties will start from a place far away from their real positions. They go further back in order to lose less while compromising with the other party.

Two parties with little problems between them may become major enemies if they focus on the compromise process.

> **⚠ Example**
>
> After eight years, Iranian people successfully elected Mr Rouhani, a well-known moderate politician, as their president.
>
> They are optimistic for the prosperous future of their land, and one major conflict that the new government is planning to manage is with United States.
>
> After the election and long before receiving the keys to the office, there started many fervent debates in the US Congress on more sanctions against Iran.
>
> Any negotiation with Iranians will sure include reducing US limitations against Iran, so it is much better to start with a bag full of sanctions.
>
> On the other hand, the other party is also filling his bag.

> Both parties are going further and further away from each other, in order to prepare to come close to each other! That is the irony of compromise.

The example above clearly shows the most radical problem of going to negotiation with our minds fixed on compromising.

> ✔ **Practice**
> - Have you ever compromised in a conflict situation?
> - What were the results (short-term and long-term)?

6.3.5 Collaborating

Collaborating is absolute assertiveness and absolute cooperativeness. In this style, you will never back down from your interests; in the meanwhile, you always insist on the other party gaining everything they want. (It seems a bit odd, doesn't it?)

The people with this mindset never will accept a compromised solution. They do not rest until they reach a true win-win solution.

> **❝ Quote**
>
> I can accept anything, except what seems to be the easiest for most people: the halfway, the almost, the just-about, the in-between.
>
> — Ayn Rand

Collaborating requires both parties to work together and discuss the issues in depth. They have to discover the roots of their partner's concerns and the exact needs they may have, as well as helping the other party to understand exactly the same about them.

It is essential for this process to spend time and energy to learn and understand the other party. This is the only style in which all the parties learn and educate. They learn themselves and educate the other party.

> Collaborating depends profoundly on effective learning, based on effective listening and effective observing.

It is an arduous task to expect others to give everything completely to their adverse party, especially if the other party is an absolute assertive person.

We have thousands of years of experience in the art of killing and capturing. We are the most adept creatures at fighting and surviving. The survival instinct has been engraved deep inside our souls; therefore, it is most natural for us to always think in a win-lose approach. Actually, for centuries, we have been thinking exactly that way, and most of us still do.

We are amazingly competitive creatures. This is one thing that we have learned and never let go. That is because we have witnessed, many times, that those who let go lost brutally. That is the core reason of our competitive approach, even when we are going for a negotiation to achieve a mutually beneficial solution. We mostly go to negotiations just to win and make the adverse party gain as less as possible, or even lose as much as possible.

> The competing mindset:
> ***In order for me to win, you have to lose.***

As mentioned in section 6.1, A Look Back, humankind successfully developed a conflict management mechanism called the adversary system. However, the competitive mindset was still strongly present.

The concept of winner and loser was embedded into the adversary system. The sole responsibility of the judge was, and still is, to find if the defendant is guilty or not. If the defendant is identified as guilty, he or she loses, and the prosecutor wins; if the defendant is identified as not guilty, it is the prosecutor who has lost, unless they go through a plea bargain, which in nature is a lost situation for the prosecutor, because they could not come up with enough evidence against the defendant, or they could not find what the defendant knows and can witness, without his or her help.

In 1948, Morton Deutsch brought up a very interesting issue. At the time, he was working with Dr Kurt Lewin (MIT) on a research project in which Dr Lewin believed that the way we treat other people in our surroundings depends on if we perceive them as "allies" or "obstacles".

It was Deutsch who was first to argue the merit of the assumption that every conflict is competitive. He came to this belief that it was not necessary to view a conflict as a win-lose situation.

He developed his work on categorising conflicts in two distinctive groups: "competitive conflicts" and "cooperative conflicts" (Deutsch 1983). Deutsch developed the idea of win-win solutions.

Although this may be one of the first appearances of this concept in Western literature, it has a very long presence in other societies. In the Eastern philosophy, for example, there is always a clear intention to lead people towards the virtue of giving and being gentle, thus controlling and balancing the competitive nature of human beings.

> **" Quote**
>
> 谷神不死
>
> 是謂玄牝
>
> 玄牝之門
>
> The life-giving valley is a heavenly example of constant change and sustainable life.
>
> So true it defines the complex concept of femininity.
>
> Profound and mysterious it is. Acceptance opens doors.
>
> — *Laozi, Dao De Jing, chapter 6*

Openness, accepting the magnitude of the universe, and having the capacity for infinities help you develop and prosper. Openness expands the thought; the mind will utilise the knowledge of the universe only as much as its capacity and readiness (Laozi, chapter 7). Therefore, to fully understand the collaborating mode, you need to be free of judgements and open your mind to expand your ability to learn.

> ✅ *Practice*
>
> - Write down any conflict situation in which you have collaborated.
> - What did you learn about your adverse parties in each conflict?

6.4 Dos and Don'ts

In the last chapter, we learned about five distinctive styles that people usually employ to deal with a conflict. It does not mean that people use only one specific style in their entire life to deal with conflict. People adapt, learn, and change, and more importantly, the circumstances differ greatly from one to another.

A man may avoid conflicts with his wife in the home, even if he has a very competitive management style in his workplace and bosses everyone around.

The learning of the five styles also does not mean that you have to choose the best style from them. You are like a chess player in your real life. You need all your pieces, regardless of whether it is a pawn, a bishop, or a queen.

> For effectively manage conflict, you need to master each style perfectly.

You have to learn how to be an extremely competitive person, how to fight, and how to order people around, regardless of their feelings. Seems cruel? Of course, it is; life is cruel.

It is also important to learn how to avoid a situation effectively and how not to get involved. You cannot believe how hard it is to shut these blabbering mouths of ours.

> **❝ Quote**
>
> Courage is what it takes to stand up and speak; courage is also what it takes to sit down and listen.
>
> — Winston Churchill

It is also very important, even crucial, to learn how to give and how to be merciful. Giving is not as easy as you may think it is. To hand over something dear and give it up is challenging, especially when you want absolutely nothing in return and you truly believe in this course of action.

Compromising is also a technique that you should learn to master. There may be situations in which you have to compromise. In this case, you'd better know how to bargain effectively and efficiently; otherwise, you will lose all your points in the game and gain little in return.

Finally yet importantly, you have to be the true master of collaborating. This is the most onerous task and takes lots and lots of practice. You need to learn the art of listening and observing, and be adept at effective answering. Your eyes and ears should be wide open and observe each and every single movement and word.

> **❝ Quote**
>
> I remind myself every morning: Nothing I say this day will teach me anything. So if I'm going to learn, I must do it by listening.
>
> — *Larry King*

The following will help to build a framework on when to use (or not use) a specific style.

6.4.1 Avoiding

The genius idea behind the avoiding style is to clear out, run for your life! Although it has a sense of escaping, avoiding is an effective conflict management style, if used properly.

You are walking down a street and want to pass an alley when you see a huge man standing in the entrance of the alley, playing with his knife. He sneers at you and calls you names. Which one of the conflict management styles will you probably use? I hope you have all them in mind, because it is not the time to ask the big guy to wait a minute while you search your book for a proper course of action.

A sound mind will order you to swallow your pride and avoid the situation. It is better to find another way and not pass this alley. If your pride gets the better of you, just remember to reflect and find out where you have done wrong, while you are lying down on a hospital bed.

Avoiding also helps you buy time and gather your wits when confronting an emotionally challenging situation. When your adverse party is very emotional and angry, it is not the time to sit down and discuss the philosophy of Thales of Miletus that whether water is the *arche* (a Greek word that means "origin") or not.

There are two important and competing forces in human beings: logic and emotion. They both compete for the limited resources of the human brain. When the emotions are high and you are boiling with rage, it takes over the logic and consumes every resource of your brain, leaving your logic to rot in its loneliness.

When the emotions are boiling, there is no place for logic. So do not bother reasoning with your angry child, or upset wife, or crazy husband.

If you open the door and find your furious wife, asking you why you are coming home so late, it is not the place to calculate the costs of your household and reason that you have to work overtime to be able to put some bread on the table. You will definitely lose your bed tonight. This is exactly what the spare rooms are for; they are safe havens for you to retreat into and wait for the morning to come.

When the emotions are high, you need to avoid the situation and let it cool down. You shall not use your extraordinary logical reasoning. You need to use emotions to deal with emotional situations and try to calm your partner down. You need to bring water to the fire, not logs, for heaven's sake.

On the other hand, it is not always advisable to avoid conflicts. When your wife asks you to have a talk to your son, you cannot and should not avoid the situation. You cannot even ask for other family members to come to the rescue. This is your son, and it is your responsibility to manage the conflict.

Moreover, you need a long-term solution for the problem. Today you avoid the situation and turn your back; what about tomorrow, or the day after? Someday, someone has to do something.

You may well avoid when the emotions are high; however, you need to come back and face the problem. The solution surely is not avoiding.

Avoiding never brings commitment. People will never entrust avoiding people with anything, because they know they will turn their back and avoid any difficulty in the way. The excessive use of avoiding only brings loneliness.

Table 1 summarises the usage guide for the avoiding style.

Conflict Style	When to Use	When Not to Use
Avoiding	• The issue is trivial and unimportant • Emotions are soaring high, and there is a need to calm the situation • Costs are more than benefits	• It is your responsibility to manage the conflict • There is a need for a long-term solution • There is a need for commitment

Table 1. Conflict Style: Avoiding

6.4.2 Competing

Competitiveness is a force inside that pushes you forward towards your goals. It blinds the eyes to everything else, just like the blinders used on racehorses to make them see only the front.

Because of the nature of competition, in which only winning is important, not anything else, you may probably neglect the other's interests or needs, and you may say or do something which may bring bad feelings for your adverse party (your partner in conflict).

One important characteristic of feelings, especially bad feelings, is that they have the nasty habit of engraving them into our memories.

When we experience something, the account of that incident, specifically, the sensual information, will be stored in our memory system. When this experience involves an emotional feeling, it will have deeper impacts.

The stored information has little to do with our usual senses of sight, hearing, and so on; rather, you will remember the *feeling* that you experienced directly through your heart and brain. It may be a happy memory of a Christmas party, or a bitter melancholy of an accident. The bitterness has this irritating habit of reminding us, again and again.

Our sensors can pick a single black dot in a white canvas with absolute ease. During our day-to-day activities and our encounters with different people, we catch negative feelings almost instantly. When your boss says something to you, the mind races to find all the black marks it possibly can. We absorb bitterness with an absolute eagerness, as if we are born hungry for sadness.

Therefore, it is critical to think rigorously on every single word we utter and any movement of our body parts. Doing this may be ignored while in competing mode. In this mode, you may see and hear nothing but yourself. You may very easily hurt someone emotionally, or even physically, very well depend on the degree of your competitiveness.

In complex situations, you need to observe and consider every possible angle, and there is a need to ask for other people's opinion and point of views. That is exactly why competing is not advisable when you are managing people and running a business, because an organisation is a complex system of different people, and you need to deliberate carefully and consider every possibility.

With all the dangers this assertive style brings to the table, it has its own use, of course. If you are short in time and the time frame is narrow, you do not have the luxury of long debates and profound reasoning. When the army decides to capture a target, it is the general who gives the order. He does not form the council of his men to debate on the issue.

"Oh, by the way, let's see what everybody has to say, we are a democracy, if I remember right!" Of course, the general will seek the counsel of his advisers, but there are times that he must decide with whatever information he has at the time. He cannot wait; time flies during such grave encounters.

Sometimes you may be trapped between two evils, a dilemma; you may wonder which of the two unfavourable alternatives could possibly be selected.

A president may feel in a quandary whether to shoot down a hijacked airplane full of passengers, or wait for them to crash the plane inside the metropolitan area. All the advisers will be divided into two groups and discuss the pros and cons. However, in the end, it is the president who has to decide and force his decision for an immediate execution.

There may also be some issues that have grave importance to you, for example, the safety of your loved ones. In this case, you will hardly listen to anybody else and will do whatever it takes to ensure their safety. You will certainly compete to the end, until you still have a bit of hope. After that, and if you lose the hope, you will shift to other styles, whether it be avoiding, accommodating, or even compromising.

When the opponent is weak and not competent, it is easy for us to impose ourselves upon them, but if they are as strong as we are, or even stronger than us, then a sound mind will decide differently.

I was always fascinated by rather astonishing behaviours of male animals during mating seasons. During the autumn, the male moose believe it is a very good time for mating, so they start with their ritual bloody battles and astounding fights to compete for the unfortunate female.

They go back and forth and drive their antlers into the opponent's skull, trying to persuade him to submit. After a while, they are all bleeding, because they are all strong, and they cannot arrange for a grown-up meeting to discuss the situation man-to-man.

We humans are often the same. We go back and forth and bump our heads together (figuratively speaking, of course!) and continue to fight until we drop down, panting. Thank you, raging hormones.

This appetite of ours (to compete) drives us to aggressive behaviours, even towards our own flesh and blood. When your wife ask you to have a word with your prodigal son, you may get angry with him and even raise your voice to teach him some respect and prove your dominance.

He may be scared of you for that and may obey you for a while, at least in your presence. However, this aggression will only drive him underground and make his behaviour more surreptitious. He may start hiding from you and try not to reveal his secrets to you. This way, you have only ensured the considerable loss of your management domain.

Also, there may emerge another negative dynamic inside your family. After your rage, your spouse may strongly feel she should go to the son and soothe him down, to mollify his anger and animosities. This social dynamic will grow them together and will construct a defensive wall between you and them.

Conflict Style	When to Use	When Not to Use
Competing	• The time frame is narrow • There is no good solution; each one has some negative points • Others are not competent • The issue has an extreme importance for you	• The issues are complex • There is a need to receive more information and other's opinion • Others are competent • There is a need for a long-term solution • There is a need for commitment

Table 2. Conflict Style: Competing

6.4.3 Accommodating

This is an extreme style, and therefore, like the other extreme style (competing), it should be handled with absolute care. Accommodating entails giving up and ignoring your interests in favour of the other party.

Every accommodation is a step backward, and every time you neglect your interests is a forward step that has never been taken. In a live dynamic environment, full of givings and takings, each individual will reach an equilibrium state of its being.

For every giving, there will be a taking, and that keeps you in balance. However, if you just give, and never take anything back, it requires being an absolute saint for you not to reach the point of complete destruction.

A housewife who is accepting the role of managing the household and nothing more will probably fill her day with washing, cleaning, cooking, tidying up, and watching TV. If her partner does not provide her with enough emotional support, and if she could not manage to arrange some time-outs for herself, or be with her friends, depression will gradually develop.

She sees her partner's busy schedule and notices how he has many co-workers. She may witness his rise inside his place of work and may think she has not achieved a single thing, except preparing his lunch box.

You have to have something for your own; you need to take something back from life. It may be the love and affection of your family; it may be the free time you may have to write a book; it could be your joyful time with your friends. It does not matter what you take, as long as you are happy with it.

> You need to take something back from life.

If you work in a company and your boss demands more time and energy from you, day after day, you should consider your life as a whole and not just your career. It is acceptable for you to obey the rules in your business environment and spend more time than normal, if asked from time to time. Notice the term *from time to time*; it is fundamentally different from the term *always*.

If you always give in, and they always ask you to sacrifice your family and life for the good of the company, you must one day sit down and start thinking, I mean really thinking. What are you losing, and what are you gaining? Never forget to look at the big picture. Otherwise, you may find yourself defending your ever-decreasing territory in your company, while losing your family completely.

Never forget, there are always people much younger than you, with more recent university degrees, with no family and no obligations, and demanding much less salary; fully ready to get your job. Therefore, if you are planning to win your job by sacrificing what you have at hand, namely your time and your family, it is more probable that you will lose on both sides.

Except if you could reach high enough in your company, which in that case, you will lose only yourself and your family, nothing more.

> Wrong belief:
> Family is always there; it is my job that I am losing.

On the other hand, if the issue has little importance to you, you may well accommodate to your adverse party. Let's say you are planning a summer vacation with your partner, and you have no specific place in mind. You could easily gain a brownie point (or two) by a simple accommodation: "Whatever you decide, honey!" and with cream on top: "There is nothing in the world more important than your happiness" (you naughty boy!).

> If you go in a battle with little knowledge
> and skills, the only thing that you
> will succeed in will be failure.

There may also be situations in which you may not be that competent or knowledgeable. In these cases, you have a great opportunity to successfully destroy your reputation and prestige by going further with the conflict and start discussing the issue. If you go in a battle with little knowledge and skills, you definitely will be defeated, because you have not foreseen every possible angle and you have not prepared yourself for the situation.

On the other hand, you should not back away if your value system is at stake. Our value system is a comprehensive set of moral laws that governs the rights and wrongs of decisions.

As soon as we come into this world, we start grasping the meanings and concepts around us. Further on, with each decision and action, we receive reactions from society and the environment, and we learn what is wrong and what is right. This experience grows gradually into an exhaustive (and ever-evolving) value system.

You can never back down from one of your values. If you do, it contradicts the very definition of *value*, which is the core belief of what is right and what is wrong.

When you give up a value, you have narrowed the boundary in which you live as a human being. Even the most immoral people have some sort of value system for them: "beliefs about what is right and wrong and what is important in life" (*Oxford Advance Learner's Dictionary* 2010).

Moreover, when you undoubtedly believe you are right, you must not accommodate. Accommodating means giving up your position and accepting your adverse party's position, which should not happen if you truly believe you are right. In this case, you should definitely use another style.

The dos and don'ts of this style have been summarised in the following table:

Conflict Style	When to Use	When Not to Use
Accommodating	• The issue has little importance to you • Your knowledge or skill regarding the issue is low • You are planning for a give and take • You have no power	• Your values are at stake • You are absolutely sure that you are right

Table 3. Conflict Style: Accommodating

6.4.4 Compromising

Wildlife can always be a source of inspiration. You might have seen bighorn rams fighting (thanks to the TV technology; not that we go out of our steel and cement cities to enjoy the nature). They go some steps back, and when they think the distance is far enough, they charge towards each other, bang their heads good and hard, and lock their curly horns: a very nice demonstration of a competing style.

The problem escalates when two males come to this "business meeting", with almost the same powers and huge egos. All hell breaks loose. They ram their heads again and again. There seems to be no compromise in their vocabulary; win or lose, that is the only way. They go until they drop down.

It would be wise to conclude that if your opponent is as powerful as you are, do not pound your head to his; it hurts a lot. Or if you insist on trying, just for the fun of it, you can pound your heads together, just once. No wise man goes this road twice.

If you go into an alley and find it a dead-end, you will probably use this knowledge for your next travel around the city. You will, hopefully, remember that the alley is a dead-end and will not go inside again, to find out the very same fact again.

> Compromise takes place in a middle ground, not yours, not the others'.

The compromising style entails giving and taking, giving something up in order to take something you want more. It does not require extensive dialogue and exploration of the other party's interests; therefore, using this style, you can achieve an agreement in a relatively quick time. However, the important point in compromise is that the agreement is achieved in a middle ground; it is not your ground, nor is it the territory of the other party. It is a place inbetween.

Poor understanding of this delicate concept (the middle ground) has caused disasters throughout history. There are myriad examples where parties have forgotten that the middle ground is actually a no-man's land. It is a temporary settlement and is *not* a solid ground to build long-term relationships upon.

> The middle ground is actually a no-man's land.
> It is a temporary settlement.

Neither party ever forgets the scores they lost to the other side. They wanted them before, and they want them still. They have just neglected them for the sake of the things they wanted more. And there lies the root of the conflicts for the future to come, hence continuing and ongoing conflicts throughout the world.

Compromising is just one style amongst others to manage conflicts, but it has a strong hold over our way of thinking. Through the years, we have learned to fight (compete), and if we could not win in a fight, we have been forced down to accept a compromise, hence the inevitable two-step process of traditional conflict management:

1- Competing, and if that failed, then
2- Compromising

Because of the dominance of this style, along with competing, in mankind, we have used these styles extensively, and we have been cheerful that we are solving the conflicts.

The situation between China and Taiwan, Israel and Palestine, Turkish-Kurdish issues in Turkey, US and Iraq, US and Afghanistan, US and Iran, China and Xinjiang, and much more conflicts are among these cases in which the combination of competing and compromising have been used for years to no avail. Yet still we can see the usage of the word "compromise" as a replacement for "conflict management" in political and management literature.

> **Quote**
>
> Discourage litigation. Persuade your neighbours to *compromise* whenever you can. As a peacemaker, the lawyer has superior opportunity of being a good man. There will still be business enough.
>
> — Abraham Lincoln, Persuade Your Neighbors to Compromise, 1991

> **Quote**
>
> The ability to *compromise* is not a diplomatic politeness toward a partner but rather taking into account and respecting your partner's legitimate interests.
>
> — Vladimir Putin, Person of the Year 2007, Putin Q&A: Full Transcript, 2007

> **Quote**
>
> But just as they did in Philadelphia when they were writing the Constitution, sooner or later, you've got to *compromise*. You've got to start making the compromises that arrive at a consensus and move the country forward.
>
> — Colin Powell, No Regrets: about Backing Obama 2010

> **❝ Quote**
>
> Let us sit down at the negotiating table. Let us put aside all preconditions. Let us work together to achieve the historic *compromise* that will end our conflict once and for all.
>
> — Benjamin Netanyahu (Remarks by Israeli Prime Minister Netanyahu and US President Obama at Joint Press Conference in Jerusalem 2013)

> **❝ Quote**
>
> That is why everyone in politics, and we do it, must make sure that they do not depend on one single interest group. A good *compromise* is one where everybody makes a contribution.
>
> — Angela Merkel (Transcript of Angela Merkel interview 2005)

Competing and compromising have long replaced the art of conflict management in our mindsets. Our first action, most of the times, is to impose ourselves over the other party. We bang our heads until there is no life left in our body. Then we forcefully move towards compromising.

Then again, during the compromise, we try our best to lose less to and gain more from the other party. We still compete, even when we are compromising.

Thousands of years of evolution have engraved competing as the sole means of survival. Dinosaurs could not survive that way. We had to learn more.

> We are born hunters.

Compromising does not bring a long-term commitment; it just helps to reach an agreement quickly. In this regard, it is crucial to understand the distinction between agreement and commitment. Of course, by law, the parties should be committed to whatever they have agreed upon, but there is a difference between what you ought to do and what you feel and want to do.

You may well be bound by law to your agreements, yet you will always have this nagging feeling about the points you lost in order to achieve the current agreement.

In complex situations, compromise is very hard to achieve. A complex situation consists of a multitude of components with various relations; therefore, it is rather challenging to decide which parts to keep, and which parts to give up as a give-and-take process in compromising.

> Seeking a compromise in a complex conflict is like wandering in a desert, running for mirages.

It is almost impossible to give up a part of a complex system, as all the parts and components are systematically related to each other, and lack of any part will jeopardise the whole system. This compromise might never be reached, and even if it could be reached (through deception, threats, and so on), it will never be maintained in the long term.

Conflict Style	When to Use	When Not to Use
Compromising	• There is a power balance between two parties • The goals are obviously incompatible and inconsistent, and there is a need for a middle ground • A quick solution is needed	• One party is more powerful than the other one • The issue is complex • There is a need for a long-term solution • Your values are at stake

Table 4. Conflict Style: Compromising

6.4.5 Collaborating

Collaborating is constructed upon dialogue, listening, and learning. It requires both parties to devote considerable time and energy to discuss the issue in detail and find the very root of the conflict, listen to the other party's requirements, and learn their interests.

This is an extremely time-consuming process in which both parties should be willing to participate and collaborate. Both should be devoted to the process and believe in the true win/win solution.

> ⚠ *Example*
>
> An old man was deep in thought, sitting on a bench in the park. "What are you thinking about, George?" his friend asked.
>
> "Do you know the difference between the left wing of a crow and the right one?" responded George.
>
> His friend pondered over the riddle and answered, "Obvious! The left wing is *more* the same as the right one"!

That may be droll, but believe it or not, there are also two kinds of win-win solutions (as well as two kinds of wings): "I win completely/you win less" and "You and I win completely." The latter is the kind I prefer to call the true win/win solution.

The first one is a poor adaptation of the concept of win-win with a competing mindset. (Do you remember our ever-present survival instinct?)

You may find it hard to believe, but you will observe such approaches if you pay close attention to people's behaviours. You can reveal such positions by observing the amount of time and energy your adverse party devotes to the process, and note at which point they are convinced they have reached the end of discussion.

> In a true win-win situation, neither party will be convinced unless the other one is completely satisfied, not the other way around.

In a collaborating style, we try to learn the other party's interests and goals, and seek to find solutions to satisfy them completely. Doing so, we also expose ourselves and bring everything on the table to facilitate the same process for the other party to easily find our needs and goals. There is no need to make them struggle in this endeavour.

Both parties openly discuss the issues, their sensitivities, likes and dislikes, goals, and so on. Neither one is afraid of a back-stabbing action, no worries that the information they are offering freely may be used against them.

It is obvious that for a collaborating style to work, both parties should be willing to collaborate; otherwise, the apprehensions will be there, and both parties may act very protective and not reveal their needs, even they will hide them in the fear of being used against them.

> Compromise has a negative connotation.

This style is the only conflict management style in which the problems are discussed in full detail with no prejudice, and both parties will learn. Neither one will be forced to neglect or give up any interest or point; therefore, the whole process shapes around positive thinking and positive learning, completely unlike compromise, which conveys a negative sense of losing something.

Accordingly, whenever a complex issue is at hand, the only way to go forward is by collaborating, because all the aspects and angles shall be observed and discussed, and both parties should completely learn the exact needs of the other party.

Complex situations need to be fully analysed and discovered. If even a single point remains unclear, it will be a possible seed for future conflicts and further disagreements. And exactly because of this deep analysis and mutual understanding, the process brings long-term commitments and alliances.

Conflict Style	When to Use	When Not to Use
Collaborating	• The issues are complex • There is a need to receive more information and other's opinion • Others are competent • There is a need for a long-term solution • There is a need for commitment	• The time frame is narrow • The other party is not competent or not willing to collaborate • Your values are at stake

Table 5. Conflict Style: Collaborating

7

The Conflict Management Process

7.1 Overview

In previous sections, we discussed the five major styles of conflict management and the proper use of them in real-life problems. In Table 6, you can find all the five styles in one place.

As mentioned before, it does not mean that we have to select one best style among others; they are all critical pieces in our chessboard.

Conflict Style	When to Use	When Not to Use
Avoiding	<ul><li>The issue is trivial and unimportant</li><li>Emotions are soaring high, and there is a need to calm the situation</li><li>Costs are more than benefits</li></ul>	<ul><li>It is your responsibility to manage the conflict</li><li>There is a need for a long-term solution</li><li>There is a need for commitment</li></ul>

Conflict Style	When to Use	When Not to Use
Competing	<ul><li>The time frame is narrow</li><li>There is no good solution; each one has some negative points</li><li>Others are not competent</li><li>The issue has an extreme importance for you</li></ul>	<ul><li>The issues are complex</li><li>There is a need to receive more information and other's opinion</li><li>Others are competent</li><li>There is a need for a long-term solution</li><li>There is a need for commitment</li></ul>
Accommodating	<ul><li>The issue has little importance to you</li><li>Your knowledge or skill regarding the issue is low</li><li>You are planning for a give and take</li><li>You have no power</li></ul>	<ul><li>Your values are at stake</li><li>You are absolutely sure that you are right</li></ul>
Compromising	<ul><li>There is a power balance between two parties</li><li>The goals are obviously incompatible and inconsistent, and there is a need for a middle ground</li><li>A quick solution is needed</li></ul>	<ul><li>One party is more powerful than the other one</li><li>The issue is complex</li><li>There is a need for a long-term solution</li><li>Your values are at stake</li></ul>

Conflict Style	When to Use	When Not to Use
Collaborating	• The issues are complex • There is a need to receive more information and other's opinion • Others are competent • There is a need for a long-term solution • There is a need for commitment	• The time frame is narrow • The other party is not competent or not willing to collaborate • Your values are at stake

Table 6. Conflict Style: Overall Summary

Although for an idealistic mind, the collaboration style seems very appealing, all about dialogues, mutual understanding, world peace, and all the good things, it is not always the case in the real world.

For the collaboration process to work effectively, it is crucial for all the parties to be willing to collaborate; otherwise, the process will seriously backfire.

You cannot open your heart freely and expose yourself to people when you are not sure of their trustworthiness. It takes time and effort to build such a relationship and trust to enable both parties to be free of worry and doubt.

> Trust is the key ingredient for a successful collaborating process.

The conflict-management styles must be used together in an absolute harmony towards the final goals. One may start with a particular style, change to the next one, and continue with another style.

> ⚠ *Example*
>
> Your child needs dialogue and understanding, as well as discipline and restraint. You should talk to her and listen carefully to what she has to say. You need to learn her underlying needs and interests.
>
> On the other hand, you are the parent in this relationship and need to develop her skills and improve her behaviours. She needs to learn discipline and respect.
>
> Sometimes you have to punish a bad behaviour, and in these cases you are using the competing style, insisting on your position and ignoring, although temporarily, your child's feelings.
>
> However, remember the usage guide for competing. The competing style does not bring long-term commitments; therefore, you need to shift to the accommodating style as soon as you are done with your competing, to cool down her emotions.
>
> Also, remember the usage guide for accommodation. Your position is right, so you should not give into her demands. You only need to mollify her, getting her ready for the next step, which is the collaborating style.
>
> You talk to her and explain your position. You explain why you think this position is the right one. You demonstrate the errors in her way and the negative outcomes she may receive in her life.

> You need to construct a solid commitment for her to reach the same belief as you do. You cannot force your beliefs into her mind. She has to reach them herself.

The conflict management process is, in fact, a process. It is not a single action, rather a series of well-planned, well-performed operations. The conflict itself is a dynamic phenomenon; therefore, the process of managing it has also a dynamic nature. The process evolves and develops as your mind evolves, and as your adverse party's mind changes.

To manage a conflict effectively, you need to be extremely observant and be an effective listener. The other party's words must be captured in full detail. All the movements, even a slight gesture, have to be observed with absolute attention.

The whole process of conflict management is a complex combination of forward charging, retreating, soothing, accepting, rejecting, mollifying, talking, convincing, and satisfying.

This conflict management process must be performed in harmony, like a well-balanced, elegant dance. Every step has its own meaning, and every move should be performed in its proper time. The performance should be in complete coordination with the other party, or else the whole dance will be spoiled.

> The conflict management process must be performed like a well-balanced, elegant dance.

✅ **_Practice_**

- Write down any conflict situation in which you have compromised when you were not supposed to.
- What were the results?
- What did you gain?
- What did you lose?
- Identify those situations in which you have competed when you were not supposed to.
- What were the results?
- What did you gain?
- What did you lose?

7.2 Change Management Process

The whole difference between a beautiful dance and a conflict-management process is the difference in goals between partners. In a dance, both parties have the same goal and coordinated routines, whereas in a conflict-management process, each party has its own goal and its own perceived reality. Therefore, for the process to be performed in complete harmony, each party tries to change the other one towards its own interests and goals, and there lies one of the major difficulties of the process: *the resistance to change.*

Everything in the universe is in an equilibrium state. One might observe an object to be in a moving state, or it may be seen as a fixed and not-moving object. Nevertheless, it is in its own equilibrium state and demonstrates inertia towards changing its state.

Opposing forces of nature (yin and yang) keep everything in a balanced position. Therefore, moving something from its equilibrium state and changing its position requires a very fine art of change management.

Change management is a major field with an extensive collection of invaluable resources and theories developed by various scholars and management professionals. There are numerous frameworks dedicated to illustrate and facilitate the understanding of the process of change management.

In 1947, Dr Kurt Lewin (Lewin 1947) introduced a three-step model to demonstrate the process in which change can occur. This three-step model actually laid the foundation for change management theories and frameworks.

As Lewin presents, every change-management process can be divided into three phases: unfreeze, move, and freeze. The first step is to unfreeze the current status quo and the balanced equilibrium. Unfreezing turns the intractable, fixed object into a more malleable state.

The second step in the process of change management is to move towards the desired situation: the next equilibrium state. This is the most delicate part of the process, and moving an unfrozen, hence more acquiescent, object must be done in absolute care and diligence.

The final step is to finalise the new equilibrium state by freezing the object in its new situation, hence fixing it and maintaining the equilibrium.

In conflict management, we need to shape our adverse party's beliefs towards what we want. Therefore, we use the term *shape* instead of *move*, as it better describes our work in managing the conflict.

> Conflict management process:
> A delicate change management process of
> **Unfreeze – Shape – Refreeze**

The conflict management process is, in fact, a very fine and delicate change management process. To reshape your adverse party, you need to first unfreeze his or her mind, shape it, and then refreeze it, all with absolute care and uppermost precision.

> ✓ *Practice*
>
> - Consider one poor fellow for your field practice. A family member or a close friend is the best choice because this person has the least defence mechanism against you (hopefully).
> - Identify one change goal to achieve with the person you have chosen. The smaller the change, the better. It is a spiral, remember; it starts very small and grows gradually.

7.2.1 Unfreeze

For every change to be successfully implemented, we need to first overcome the initial inertia and the resistance to change. We need to turn the other party's state from a solid and resisting state to a more tractable one, hence the term *unfreeze*.

Turning a moving car can be done by simply turning the steering wheel, but if the car is not moving and is stopped, it will be a bit harder to move it around.

To move, first we have to overcome the inertia and the tendency to maintain the status quo. We need to manipulate the forces that keep the object in its place, adamantly refusing to budge.

In every equilibrium state, there are multiple opposing forces that help maintain the equilibrium state. These forces push the object to different directions in such a way that the total outcome keeps the object in its current position.

> ⚠ **Example**
>
> You can put a wooden block on an inclined plane in such a way that it keeps still and does not slide down. In this equilibrium position, the gravity force drags the block down the slope while the friction between the block and the surface tries to keep it still in its current position.

To overcome this inertia, we should strengthen some forces and weaken others in such a way that the outcome of all the forces directs the object in the desired direction.

> **⚠ Example**
>
> In the previous example, to make the block move, you need to either increase the force of gravity (by increasing the slope), help it (by pushing it down), or decrease the friction force (by using oil beneath the block).
>
> Either way, the block will start moving downwards.

In every conflict situation, both parties have their own perception of reality and their own set of goals and interests that drive them forward to achieve these goals.

In their current beliefs and the direction each of the parties is pursuing, all the parties have reached an equilibrium state in which there are multiple forces that keep each party in its current position.

One characteristic of the human mind is that it clings to its belongings (say, thoughts and beliefs) rather obsessively. This is a natural process in a human mind: to develop understandings and theories based on available information and therefore shape its desires and interests.

This is also inherent: that the mind keeps its belongings (thoughts and beliefs) and protects them against any threats from the outside world, the very same survival instinct of human beings.

Therefore, whenever you receive anything contradictory and inconsistent with your thoughts and beliefs, you have reached a conflict situation. Your mind will defend itself against any contradicting argument, and you will resist changing your beliefs, hence the resistance to change.

That is why every conflict situation evokes negative and discomforting feelings, thus the definition:

> **Conflict is a discomforting difference.**

The defence mechanism of the human brain resists any intruding idea. Therefore, it is essential to diminish this defensive fortification before you directly attack the stronghold. The unfreeze phase in the change management process tries to do the very same serious task.

You might use a combination of styles in order to lower the defences. It is exactly like a battle; you may attack the gate or the bowmen on the walls, or flank the guarding towers, or even attack the resources.

> A book to consider:
> *The Art of War,* Sun Tzu

This phase can be about war and destruction; it can also be about building and construction. If you are in a competing style and the other party's interests and goals are not important to you, you could use this phase to lower the fences and destroy the defences, so they could better accept your way and have nothing to oppose.

On the other hand, if you are in a collaborating style, this phase is all about constructing a strong trust between two parties.

To build a new house, you need to first clear out the weeds, remove the boulders, and prepare the land. So you attack and destroy those defences that are destructive, causing doubt and opposing the trust.

> ✅ **Practice**
>
> - Doing the previous assignment, now you have a subject in mind to change towards a goal you have identified.
> - Now, write down as many defence mechanisms as you can identify that your subject may have against your goal.
> - What do you think they may say against your proposal?
> - What do you think they may think (and may hardly say) against your proposal?
> - What are their worries? Discover them; explore them, listen, observe, learn.
> - Which of these defences are destructive against a collaborating style?
> - How can you build trust for yourself in their minds regarding the goal you have?
> - What time frame do you think is necessary to build such trust?

7.2.2 Shape

Completion of the unfreeze phase lays the groundwork for the next critical phase: *shape*. In this phase, you have successfully changed your adverse party to a more malleable state; now you can start working on the change itself and shape them into your desired form.

This phase requires absolute tact and considerable attention, as well as the complete understanding of the other party. You need to be able to talk in their language and be sufficiently adept at their own specific logic.

Your logic is your way of thinking, which may not be the same as theirs. The final goal is that they understand and believe that your position is the right one, and that can only be achieved if they understand and acknowledge the reasoning you are providing.

This process of convincing requires resolving all their worries and doubts, as their final lines of defence; then the ground is ready to plant the seeds. These seeds need to grow on their own; you do not need to push them out. Nature never pushes any plant to grow faster; everything needs its time to become ripe and mature. Their minds, as well, need time to process the new information and analyse it thoroughly, or else they may not commit in the long term.

> Change management is done through planting and nourishing.
> **Patience is a virtue.**

To form an idea, you have to plant the seeds and take care of the growing environment. You need to direct and lead; you should never push anything out of its place; this will disrupt the equilibrium. You need to be patient and observant. The equilibrium state cannot be forced; it must be achieved naturally and smoothly.

Remember the collaboration style (sections 6.3.5 and 6.4.5); both parties must reach full understanding and be completely satisfied.

This is the only way to ensure that the conflict does not rise again in future and cause a surprise.

If there remains a single point unsolved and the other party does not see it, and yet they agree to the outcomes, as soon as they find out about that point they will think they have been tricked into an agreement. The trust you had been working so hard for (in the unfreeze phase) will collapse, and it will be much harder to build up a shattered trust for the second time.

In fact, both parties must ensure all the issues have been discussed and all the possible angles have been observed. This is a true win-win situation. Both parties should truly believe in the fairness of the whole process; therefore, both parties should participate fully, listen effectively, and think thoroughly.

On the other hand, in a competing style, you are the one who is controlling and managing the process; the other party is only a receiver who has been groomed for this phase.

In both cases, you should be absolutely aware of the dynamic nature of the change management process. The whole process evolves through time. You may have an intended strategy for your discussions, but the realised strategy will be probably different from the one you started with.

> **" Quote**
>
> No plan survives contact with the enemy.
>
> — *Helmuth von Moltke*

During the process of conflict management, both parties learn either how to more effectively destroy (competing) or how to better satisfy (collaborating) the other one; therefore, some aspects of your original plans may be rendered useless (unrealised), and the emergent strategies will undoubtedly come up and derail your original plans to a new realised strategy.

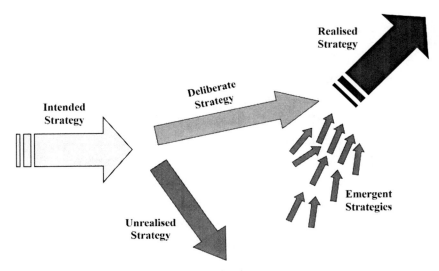

Figure 7. Realised Strategy[2]

Therefore, it is crucial to be vigilant and always have in mind that the conflict management process is continuous and dynamic. Be prepared to find the emergent issues and develop effective emergent strategies.

Do not establish special emotional bonds with your original plans and goals; they will probably change, and for the better, if the process is being managed effectively.

---

[2] Published by the permission of the publisher, Sage Publication Inc., through Copyright Clearance Centre (CCC), 222 Rosewood Drive, Danvers, MA 01923, USA from the "Strategy Formation in an Adhocracy" by Henry Mintzberg and Alexandra McHugh, *Administrative Science Quarterly* 30 (2): 160–197. doi:10.2307/2393104.

✔ Practice

- Identify the reasoning process in your mind to reach the goal that you intend to convince the other party.
- Illustrate the reasoning process as A → B → C → D → Goal.
- Find out the most fundamental point of entry (A), and identify what kind of seeds you need to plant for the A to happen in his/her mind.
- Remember: you can never mention the A; you need them to achieve A by themselves.
- While nourishing the seeds and directing the flow, effectively listen and observe. Learn the emergent issues.
- Consider revising your timetable, it may need some revisions by now.
- Revise your strategy, your reasoning flow, or even your goal if necessary.
- What have you learned about the other party?
- What are their needs?
- Where were you wrong?
- Where do you need to adjust? What do you need to modify?
- Did you achieve A? Okay → Do not move further.

7.2.3 Refreeze

You have prepared the land and have planted your seeds. Your job has not finished yet. You need to cover the planted seeds in order to protect them and nourish them. This is exactly the same in a change management process.

After unfreezing and shaping, you need to refreeze the other party in the shaped state; otherwise, it will again melt down and all the hard work will be ruined.

The human mind is a self-centred creature! It is a master in the art of survival; otherwise, we would have the same fate as our late neighbours, the dinosaurs.

The brain will usually remember what parts of its beliefs are its own and what parts are injected from outside. It always resists the injected ones, although it accommodates them sometimes. The key to change management is:

> Change will be institutionalised only through infection, not injection.

Therefore, you need to infect the other party with your ideas, hence the metaphor of planting seeds. You should not push your ideas into their minds; they will always remember this forceful push.

They need to be infected with the ideas, and then you need to nourish them and protect them. They will reach the outcome that you want eventually. The difference is, in this way, you have ensured that their own minds analyse the information and reach the conclusion; therefore, the outcome is not yours, but theirs. This time, their minds will protect this outcome rigorously.

> It is important to be patient and not celebrate too soon. There is always time for celebration.

You have to finalise the process, not by moving to the next step, but by asking the other party to go, once again, through all the issues for the last time. This way, you ensure that you have not left any unsolved issue behind. For any unsolved issue, it is much better for you to be around and resolve it rather than hide it to reach the agreement sooner. It will emerge eventually, and then, you may not be there to protect your creation.

It is important to be patient and not celebrate too soon. You have to make sure every possible way back is blocked and well secured in their minds and they will not tend to come back. There is always time for celebration. Make sure you have ticked all the boxes before going forward.

If you are in a competing style, make sure you have covered all the options. You do not want second thoughts and cold feet. If you are in a collaborating style, it is vital to ensure that your partner is completely satisfied and has not neglected any of his or her interests.

> ✓ **Practice**
>
> - You have reached A, now ensure you have secured it. Ask them to think again and find any contradicting and any opposing idea against A.
> - While leading the negotiations, concentrate on learning. The more you learn, the less surprised you will be.
> - When they reach A, accept it yourself as if it was originally their idea.
> - Again, revise your timetable and strategies.
> - After achieving A, direct and lead the flow towards B, without mentioning it directly.
> - In each sentence, learn; in each disagreement, learn; in each agreement, turn back and recheck.

- Secure B.
- Go to the next level.
- How is your timetable changing?
- How is your way of thinking changing?
- What are you learning?

8

Conclusion

It was not a target we were seeking, nor a destination; it was the way on which we started our march. Our knowledge and awareness will gradually grow more as we move ahead.

The way is like a spiral, moving upwards and outwards. It will glow brighter on each step. At first, you see tiny sparks in the dark, but going up the spiral, you will see blazing lights.

Conflict management is the art of equilibrium; it is the way of living. Conflict management will turn into our life style. The way we listen, observe, and talk will change in each step upwards: *We live the way.*

Start small; take your first steps on the way. Start practicing with people close to you. You will have errors on the way, and you will fail many times. They will forgive you if you do something wrong.

We have all had several failures before our first steps, and before we could stand on our feet and walk. So do not worry about the failures; always listen and observe. Learn from your mistakes and discover why you have failed. Which angle had you overlooked? And which need had you not satisfied?

Try your skills with close friends and family members for a while. During each step of the unfreeze-shape-refreeze, remember all about the five styles and their dos and don'ts. You will learn extensively from your practices.

After your first success at a small conflict management project, you will see the sparks. The more you go up the spiral, the brighter they become.

With each conflict managed, you will maintain the equilibrium.

You have embraced happiness.

Bibliography

Bisno, Herb. 1988. *Managing Conflict.* Newbury Park, CA: Sage Publications Inc.

Bordenn, Walter A. 1999. "A History of Justice: Origins of Law and Psychiatry." *American Academy of Psychiatry and the Law (AAPL)* 24 (2): 12–14.

Cummings, Stephen. 2002. *ReCreating Strategy.* 1. SAGE Publications Ltd.

Deutsch, Morton. 1983. "Conflict Resolution: Theory and Practice." *Political Psychology* 4 (3): 431–453.

Dues, Michael. 2010. *The Art of Conflict Management: Achieving Solutions for Life, Work, and Beyond.* Chantilly, VA: Teaching Co.

Elert, Emily. 2013. *21 Emotions for Which There Are no English Words.* 1 April. http://www.popsci.com/science/article/2013-01/emotions-which-there-are-no-english-words-infographic.

n.d. *Encyclopaedia Britannica.* Britannica.com.

Fisher, Erik A., and Sharp, Steven W. 2004. *The Art of Managing Everyday Conflict: Understanding Emotions and Power Struggles.* Praeger Publishers.

Goodpaster, Gary. 1987. "On the Theory of American Adversary Criminal Trial." *Journal of Criminal Law and Criminology* 78 (1): 146.

Hood, Thomas. n.d. Poem "Faithless Sally Brown".

Jeong, Ho-Won. 2010. *Conflict Management and Resolution.* Abingdon, Oxon: Routledge.

———. 2008. *Understanding Conflict and Conflict Analysis.* London: Sage Publications Ltd.

Kilmann, Ralph H., and Thomas, Kenneth W. n.d. *Interpersonal Conflict: Handling Behavior as Reflections of Jungian Personality Dimensions.* http://www.kilmanndiagnostics.com/interpersonal-conflict-handling-behavior-reflections-jungian-personality-dimensions.

Laozi. 400 B.C. "Dao De Jing." Chap. 2 in *Dao De Jing.*

Lewin, Kurt. 1947. "Frontiers in Group Dynamics: Concept, Method and Reality in Social Science; Social Equilibria and Social Change." *Human Relations* (Sage Publications Inc.) 1 (1): 30–40. doi:10.1177/001872674700100103.

Mercier, Hugo, and Sperber, Dan. 2011. "Why Do Humans Reason? Arguments for an Argumentative Theory." *Behavioural and Brain Sciences* 34 (2): 57-74. doi:10.1017/S0140525X10000968.

Mintzberg, Henry, and McHugh, Alexandra. 1985. "Strategy Formation in an Adhocracy." *Administrative Science Quarterly* 30 (2): 160-197. doi:10.2307/2393104.

n.d. *Newton's third law of motion.* Accessed 20 September 2013. http://en.wikipedia.org/wiki/Newton's_laws_of_motion.

2010. *Oxford Advance Learner's Dictionary.* 8th. Oxford University Press.

2007. *Person of the Year 2007. Putin Q&A: Full Transcript.* http://www.time.com/time/specials/2007/personoftheyear/article/0,28804,1690753_1690757_1695787,00.html.

1991. *Persuade Your Neighbors to Compromise.* 12 July. http://www.nytimes.com/1991/07/12/opinion/l-persuade-your-neighbors-to-compromise-218791.html.

n.d. *Plutchik Wheel.* Accessed 1 September 2013. http://en.wikipedia.org/wiki/File:Plutchik-wheel.svg.

Plutchik, Robert. 2000. *Emotions in the Practice of Psychotherapy: Clinical Implications of Affect Theories.* Washington, DC: American Psychological Association.

2010. *Powell: "No Regrets" About Backing Obama.* 21 February. http://www.cbsnews.com/8301-3460_162-6228759.html.

2013. *Remarks by Israeli Prime Minister Netanyahu and US President Obama at Joint Press Conference in Jerusalem.* http://www.jewishpost.com/news/obama-netanyahu-passover-2013.html.

Shearouse, Susan H. 2011. *Conflict 101: A Manager's Guide to Resolving Problems So Everyone Can Get Back to Work.* American Management Association (AMACOM).

n.d. *Thales of Miletus (624 BC – 546 BC).* http://en.wikipedia.org/wiki/Thales.

n.d. *The John and Muriel Higgins Home Page.* http://myweb.tiscali.co.uk/wordscape/index.html.

Thompson, Leigh L. 1998. *The Mind and Heart of the Negotiator.* Upper Saddle River, NJ: Prentice-Hall.

Toffler, Alvin. 1984. *The Third Wave.* Bantam.

2005. *Transcript of Angela Merkel interview.* 20 July. http://www.ft.com/cms/s/2/45773c4c-f945-11d9-81f3-00000e2511c8.html#axzz2cyvXdDik.

Wilmot, William, and Hocker, Joyce. 2001. *Interpersonal Conflict.* 6th. New York: McGraw-Hill.

Index

A

achieve happiness 14
achieving 10
acknowledge 157
action 29, 44, 107, 134
adaptation 17
adversary system 104
agile companies 93
agricultural society 36
ambiguity 86, 93
anger 40
argue too much 44
art of conflict management 12, 14, 139
art of equilibrium 12, 164
art of reasoning 105
art of war 155

B

bargaining process 116
being different 21
bending 17
bitter Fact 9
body language 79, 81

boss 16, 18, 93, 133
bully 36
business organising 86

C

change infection 161
change injection 161
change management 151, 157
chaos 94, 106
childhood 18, 32, 33
Churchill, Winston 111, 124
circle of life 7
climax 29, 30
commitment 127, 140, 144, 157
communication 49, 50, 53
compete/compromise 137, 139
competing mindset 121, 142
complex system 4, 129, 140
comprehending 75, 79, 80, 82
conflicting interests 11, 12, 14
conflicting needs 11, 14
conflict management 107, 124
conflict management process 149, 152
conflict positive organisation 87

conflict positive team 38
conflict resolution 107
consequences 29
control systems 4
conversion table 52
convince 106, 143, 157, 160
corporate culture 14, 33
culture 14, 62, 69, 71, 73

D

Dao De Jing 6, 7, 122
Dao of life 2, 6, 7, 8, 35
dark ages 106
decision 29
definitions 20
defy 4
depression 13, 29
Deutsch, Morton 121
development processes 94
dialectic 106
dialogue 69, 98, 136, 142, 147
dictatorship 45
dictionary 52, 62
difference between perceptions 49
difference between realities 49
differences 26
dilemma 129
direct 153, 157
discerning 80
discomfort 10, 18
discomforting 26, 27
discomforting difference 22, 40, 47, 108, 155
discover 2, 19, 27, 76, 80, 95, 106, 120, 164
discovering 80
discovery process 79
diversity 27
drowning 13

Dues, Michael 21
dynamic 46, 107, 149, 158, 159

E

effective communicator 83
effective learning 120
effective listening 77, 120
effective observing 80, 120
Einstein, Albert 96
elegant dance 149
eliminating differences 42
embrace happiness 165
emergent strategies 158
emotional needs 12
emotions 28, 29, 40, 126
endure the consequences 9
environment 12, 13, 27, 32, 34, 49, 84
equilibrium 4, 5, 11, 31
equilibrium state 6, 17, 30, 151
ever-increasing 12
evolution 8, 37, 139
existence 6
expectations 12, 25
experience 24, 53
expose yourself 147
express feelings 53
extremes 6

F

family 12, 14, 32
feelings 13, 26, 35, 36, 42, 103, 128, 154
fight or flight 40
first stages 31
flexibility 17, 93, 94
flexible job definitions 93
freedom 46
friendly environment 35

fulfilled 10

G

gap 13
giving up 17
goal 10, 21, 36, 44, 93, 100, 101, 111, 113, 128, 143, 151, 155, 157
goal incompatibilities 21
grand master 8
Greeks 105

H

happiness 1, 2, 10, 14, 114
hardship 21
hard work 13
harmony 4, 7, 12, 17, 64, 147
hearing 75
Higgins, John 67, 68
Hood, Thomas 68
human minds 4

I

imposed 14
imposing 45
industrial age society 36
inertia 151
information age society 37
interact 35
inter-dependent 35
interference 21
interpretation 26
interpreting the reality 23
intractable Situations 14
investigate the perceptions 98

J

job boundaries 93
job descriptions 93
job inputs 93

job outputs 93
journey 1
justice system 105

K

Keynes, John Maynard 118
Kilmann, Ralph H 108
King, Larry 125

L

language 52
Laozi 6, 7, 122
lead 157
learn 24, 25, 33, 160, 162
learning 142, 164
learning process 53
Lewin, Kurt 121, 151
limit 11
limited resources 91
Lincoln, Abraham 138
listen and observe 83, 164
listening 75, 77, 82, 142
logogram 52, 64
loneliness 127
long-lasting 11, 28
looking 78
love or fear 113

M

management through conflict 8
managing conflicts 12
manipulate 153
Mercier, Hugo 105
mercy 9
Merkel, Angela 139
middle ground 116, 136
monitoring 80
monitoring systems 4
mother nature 5, 8, 17

move higher 10
moving 5, 151
myths 32

N

natural phenomenon 26, 35
nature 8, 17, 29, 31
nature's eternal goal 5
negative emotions 22, 28
negative feelings 26, 42, 103, 128, 154
Netanyahu, Benjamin 139
noise 51
no-man's land 137

O

Obama, Barack 116
observing 79, 80, 82
one-way highway 42
openness 122
organisation 86
organisational mechanism 87
outlook to the world 23
overlap 86
overlapping responsibility 86

P

paradigm 25
patience 157, 161, 162
paying respect 82
Pei-Ying Lin 54
perceive 23
perception 25, 98
perception of the reality 47, 96, 151, 154
performance targets 89
persuade 106
plant the seeds 157, 160, 161
Plato 104

Plutchik, Robert 40
poles of nature 6, 7, 41
Powell, Colin 138
power 37, 111
powerful 36
promotion 12
punishments 10
purpose 44
Putin, Vladimir 138
Pythagoras of Samos 104

R

Rand, Ayn 120
realised strategy 158
reality 23, 26, 96
reasoning 75, 104, 105
resistance to change 151, 153, 154
resolution 107
resolve 107, 157
responsibilities 12, 86
root 95

S

scars 28, 31, 42
seed 27, 157, 160
seeing 78
self-experience 24
senses 23
sensory information 23
shared concept 63
shared objectives 86
sharing 50, 86
sheer bliss 11
side effects 13, 31, 43
Silverstein, Shel 113
society 34
Socrates 104
Solon 104
Sperber, Dan 105

spiral 3, 9, 29, 115, 164
spiral nature of a conflict 30
standards 93
stimulate 28
strategy revision 160, 162
strong leader 46
struggle 21
subconscious 10, 33, 104
submission 130
success 2, 10
success or failure 93
Sun Tzu 155
suppression 45
surrendering 17
survival instinct 35, 40, 45, 104, 105, 121

T

tactile information 74
Tai Chi symbol 6
take something back 132
talk too much 83
teacher 8
team 38
temporary settlement 137
Thales of Miletus 104
Thatcher, Margaret 115
thinking 75
Third Wave 36
Thomas, Kenneth W 108
time 12, 157
time frame 156
timetable 160, 162
to be or not to be? 96
Toffler, Alvin 36
true happiness 10, 11
true win-win 143, 158
trust 147, 155, 158

U

uncertainty 94
unconsciously 25
underground 130
understand 157
unfavourable alternatives 129
unhappiness 21
unmanageable 14

V

value system 134
viable 4
visual information 74
visual perception 78
vocal information 74

W

watching 79
watching carefully 80
way 2, 164
which is the best? 101
willing to collaborate 143, 147
win-lose 35, 105, 106, 121
win-win 122, 142
words 66
work environment 13, 33
workplace confusions 93
world conflicts 137
worldview 23
wounds 28

Y

yin-yang 6, 29, 35, 151

Z

Zig Ziglar 25

CPSIA information can be obtained at www.ICGtesting.com
Printed in the USA
LVOW10s2349020614

388261LV00004B/9/P